BEING NANCY

(IN A WORLD LOST IN MYSTERY)

MICHÈLE OLSON

Blessings!
Michèle Olson

Being Nancy
(In a world lost in mystery)

A Mackinac Island Story
(Book Five)
Michèle Olson

More Books by Michèle Olson
Fiction:
Being Ethel (In a world that loves Lucy)
Being Dorothy (In a world longing for home)
Being Alice (In a world lost in the looking glass)
Being Wendy (In a world afraid to grow up)
Non-Fiction:
5 Easy Steps to a Happy Birthday!
A practical, funny guide to a Happy Birthday every single year

Published by Lake Girl Publishing LLC, Green Bay, WI

www.LakeGirlPublishing.com

info@LakeGirlPublishing.com

NANCY DREW® is a registered trademark of Simon & Schuster, Inc. and is used by permission.

Scripture quotations are taken from the Holy Bible, New International Version®, NIV®. Copyright © 1973, 1978, 1984 by Biblica, Inc.™ Used by permission of Zondervan. All rights reserved worldwide. www.zondervan.com

Scripture taken from *THE MESSAGE.* Copyright © 1993, 1994, 1995, 1996, 2000, 2001, 2002. Used by permission of NavPress Publishing Group.

Library of Congress Control Number: 2024902711

ISBN 978-1-959178-02-6 (Paperback)

ISBN 978-1-959178-03-3 (eBook)

ACKNOWLEDGMENTS

Book Cover Design: Karen Kalbacher
Northern Lights and Mighty Mac Bridge Painting: Michèle
Olson
Interior Layout: Raymond A. Olson II
Editor: Sarah Lamb
Proofreader: Sophia Walsh
First Edition: 2024, printed in the U.S.A

DEDICATION

To all my fellow Nancy Drew fans. It's hard to put into words the influence this young sleuth has had on so many of us. These stories were the first seed planted for my desire to write stories with mystery and life lessons. I'm forever grateful to the Farnsworth Public Library in Oconto, Wisconsin for making these treasures available to an eager reader.

To all the "preachy girls" who share their love in real and tangible ways, every day. Special thanks to Marlene and Maxine for your prayers and encouragement.

To my husband Ray and my family Ben and Cassie, Molly and Danny, and our delightful grandsons, Jett and Jace. I love you all beyond words.

To Pastor James and Jill Kocian and the forever family at CRE8Church.com for following new visions and adventures in the name of Jesus.

To Pastor Jerry and Jeanne Bruette for your guidance and consistent walk of true faith and friendship.

To you dear readers, all my love and gratitude.

Stories Set on Mackinac Island Filled with Mystery, Mayhem, and Miracles!

This is the fifth book in my Mackinac Island Story series. The book stands on its own as a single offering; however, you will find it an even richer story if you read the first book in the series, *Being Ethel (In a world that loves Lucy)*, where we meet Piper Penn for the first time. It's set in 1979. The next book in the series is *Being Dorothy (In a world longing for home)* where Piper Penn meets a mysterious couple on the porch of the Grand Hotel, set in 1980. But are they who they seem to be? It's a story with a James Bond flair. The third book *Being Alice (In a world lost in the looking glass)* is set in 1981. A young musical genius has scars on her face that don't compare to the scars in her heart. Anyone who has ever loved a singer/songwriter and music will enjoy this story. The fourth book, set in 1982, is *Being Wendy (In a world afraid to grow up)*. A novel with a nod to Peter Pan, this story follows Wendy T. Bell, a famous author who is sure someone at her fiftieth birthday party is trying to end her career, or worse! She escapes to Mackinac Island and meets Pan Peters. Mysterious things keep happening and they don't stop!

How to help spread the news of these stories!

- Leave a review at all the big book sites. As an author, let me assure you this is super important! It helps me be found by other readers in the mass world of books.

- Give these books as gifts! Share the eBook and/or paperback versions with friends and family for birthdays and "just because." Fuel Faith with Fiction™ and join us as a #papermissionary!

- Join me on social media and share my posts. All contacts are listed in this book.

This book happened because a young girl was up bright and early on Saturday mornings to be at the Farnsworth Public Library in Oconto, Wisconsin to check out her next sleuthing adventure with Nancy Drew. Was it like that for you, too? Time to dive into this treasure. It's written with your reading enjoyment in mind—straight from my heart!

Blessings,

Michèle

I love to hear from readers! info@lakegirlpublishing.com

LESSONS OF THE LADY SLIPPER:

Growing in the northern woods and on Mackinac Island, the lady slipper reminds us of the legend about a small girl who lived long ago—a girl who saved her people from a terrible disease by listening carefully to the whispering snow, the rumbling ice, and the dancing northern lights.

CHAPTER ONE

JANUARY 1983, MACKINAC ISLAND, MICHIGAN

"*T*his is not going to be for the faint of heart. It's going to be tons of work, but I've chosen each of you because I believe you have the love and the dedication to help pull this off, even though our time is short," I say. "That, and the conversations we had."

I can't believe little 'ole me, Nancy Benson, is going to bring a Nancy Drew convention to the Grand Hotel this fall! Focus, Nancy. I have to get each of these ladies on my new committee to see how much I need them to make this happen. Bees and sheep. I need worker bees and obedient sheep who will follow me, preferably, blindly. And I need people who can keep their mouths shut to certain other people.

"Nancy, we are here for you! This is an amazing accomplishment. I can't believe you pulled all the strings so we can have a Nancy Drew convention this fall. How did you do it?"

Good. If Piper is on board, the rest will follow. I was impressed from the first moment I met Piper Penn in her Creative Lilac store, and I've seen my bank account dwindle with each of her art pieces that I can't pass up. She's not famous, but she is my favorite artist. Take that Van Gogh! Finding this shop has made living on an island this past year bearable. Nothing about coming here was what I envisioned when I said "I do" to the charming Ned Benson.

"Thanks, Piper. I was determined to make them see that Nancy Benson is the person who could build the team able to have a Nancy Drew convention at the Grand Hotel. Nancy Drew fans are the kind of people who should have their convention in this summer place of splendor!" I say.

Wow! I didn't expect a standing ovation from this small little crew, but I'll take it. I can't believe my luck and my timing. The organization originally scheduled to have their convention at The Grand for the time slot I'm so happily inheriting hit the news with scandal after scandal. Thankfully, I got word about the cancellation and didn't waste a moment taking my convention idea to the "powers that be" at the Grand Hotel. I solved their problem by having the perfect answer for their opening and they solved mine—making my dream of a gathering of Nancy Drew lovers come true. Sure, I'm no Nancy Drew expert and yes, I embellished my credentials and a few facts of why I was qualified to do this, but who doesn't do that these days? It's part of the game.

I really like these ladies, and I hope I can trust them. Nestling ourselves in Piper's studio above her shop was the respite I needed to see if they were my group. And I think they are. I've loved every art project we've done in Piper's class. It was the perfect way to get a good read on each lady while we chatted and created our masterpieces.

"You know we included your request in our last Bible study prayer time," Piper says as her gaggle of friends are all clapping and squealing.

I'm the black sheep. The rest of these sheep are regulars at Piper's weekly Bible study. Spending time in Piper's art class is enough for me. Oh boy. This is an aspect of these nice ladies I'm going to have to corral. They'll start talking about Jesus and the Bible and send our attendees running for the hills. They take their faith a little too far for my tastes. Yes, there's a God, I get it.

But some people are so heavenly minded they are no earthly good.

"Now, gals, I'm going to be blunt with you. I know you are all in the Bible study together, but this meeting is for the Nancy Drew convention, not a faith event. So, I must have your word that you will be there to do the work and not be recruiters for reading the Bible," I say.

Nice, Nancy. Way to kill a room.

"Nancy, you're right. I can only speak for myself, but I am known for talking about my faith to pretty much anyone I meet, so we need to take your guidance here. It's your event, and we all love Nancy Drew books too, so we will be on our best behavior," Piper says, looking around to the other ladies. "This meeting and the convention are all about Nancy Drew fans. I get it."

"I agree with Piper," Maxine says.

"Me too," Marlene chimes in.

"We get it," Brenda says.

"Don't worry!" Gail says, nodding.

"Oh, good. I didn't want to offend you, but, well, that's the way it has to be. I'm glad you see my point," I say.

Such nice ladies, and I know they'll be diligent workers for the convention. I need their help. I'd die if they ever found out the real reason I joined the art class was to wrangle their assistance. Thankfully, they never need to know.

"And I also need your pledge of secrecy about everything behind the scenes we are doing here. We don't need Nosy Nellies knowing every detail of how our committee works. And that includes your families and friends. All the insider ins and outs of running this convention are to be kept between us only ... do you agree?" I ask, searching each face.

They give a nod of agreement.

"I mean, I'm a private person, and we want to appear very professional in everything we do. So, good. Now, each of you will be heading up a certain aspect of the gathering, and you'll probably need to recruit a few helpers in your area. Please make sure they are people you can depend on. We have to put our best foot forward to represent our magical island. For many of these attendees, it will be their first trip here," I say.

"Nancy, I don't want to pry, but how did you pull this together so fast ... I mean, financially? Doesn't the Grand require deposits? Usually, it's only big organizations that could pull off this type of gathering," Marlene asks.

No wonder she's the one I want to run the registration and collections for attendees. She has the financial smarts I'll need.

"Not to go into too much detail, but I enlisted my husband's financial backing. Even though I'm a fifty-something, kind of newlywed ... he likes to see me happy. In fact, it's our second anniversary this week and I told him this could be my gift—helping me pull off this dream come true—to have a Nancy Drew convention. I would appreciate you not mentioning anything about finances to anyone else. This is the sort of thing I'm willing to share with you, but only confidentially. It's simply not anyone's business," I say, looking around for reactions.

I have to say whatever I can to make this make sense to these ladies without them digging any further. Seeing me happy went down the drain with Ned as soon as I stupidly said, *'til death do us part*. But they don't need to know. Once again, I get nods from around the room along with Happy Anniversary wishes.

"Nancy, we're all here for you," Brenda says. "By the way, I'm loving your new hairstyle. That blunt bob is *très chic*, as they say."

"Thanks, Brenda. Do you also notice the salt and pepper starting to show? I dare say the salt is showing up more. I've always had jet black hair, so this is truly an adjustment along with the mid-life pounds that are finding me. This fifty-plus is not for the faint of heart," I say.

"You look fantastic. Ned's a lucky guy," Marlene says.

These are the sweetest ladies. No wonder I love being with them.

"Well, you all need glasses, but thank you. Okay, back to business. I know the snow is on the ground right now and we are all lulled into the quiet of this winter wonderland, but it's January. Before we know it, October 7th, 8th, and 9th will be here. We have a lot to accomplish. I have the mailing lists of all the Nancy Drew fan clubs in every state, so we have to put together our information and registration packets and get them mailed by early April at the latest. Piper, we will count on you for the design and posters for the event pieces," I say.

It feels so good to get going.

"I can't wait to get started!" Piper says. "Don't forget, my dear friend Sister Mary- Margaret will be visiting during that time. She will be a wonderful helper, I promise. In fact, when she lived on the island, we bonded over our love of *I Love Lucy* and Nancy Drew books. She will be an asset, I promise."

Oh, boy. A nun?

"Um, should be okay. Does she wear a habit?" I'm afraid to ask, but that's a deal breaker.

"Sometimes, but more for church events. She won't wear it for the convention. It will be fine. You'll love her. She's fun, sweet, and everyone who meets her never forgets her," Piper says.

"If you say so. You sure do know everyone who lands somehow on this island," I say. "Okay, now onto assignments. Marlene, I see you running the financial registration and the books. Gail, I will need your help with speaker coordination. Brenda, I'd like you to handle the special Nancy Drew display I'm hoping to set up in the Grand Ballroom, and Maxine—I see you coordinating all the hospitality aspects for the attendees. We'll all still help each other, but if you can head up those areas, I think we can operate like a well-oiled machine."

"You hit all our areas of expertise, that's for sure," Gail says.

"I was hoping you would feel that way. You know, when Nancy Drew started sleuthing, she didn't have any formal train-ing. She trusted her instincts and learned along the way. We don't have any formal training in running a convention, but we will do fine if we all work hard and stick together. Are you with me?" I ask.

"Yes! You bet!" they all say with enthusiasm.

We seemed to have survived the awkwardness of my insistence on secrecy. At least as Bible study girls, I should be able to trust them. I mean, that has to be part of their creed or whatever. Their warm laughter is soothing that icky feeling that rushed over me when I brought up the "no God talk" policy at my convention. I must be back in their good graces.

"As we all learned from Nancy in the *Password to Larkspur Lane,* you can always expect your loyal friends to join you in schemes," I say. "Oh, and I won't be taking any salary from any convention proceeds. It will all go back into future Nancy Drew club and convention endeavors—that is, if there is any extra. I can't pay you either, but I do think you'll be able to enjoy your fellow attendees and the experts who will be speaking. I hope that's enough compensation for all your hard work," I say, once again afraid to look at their faces in case they thought this was a paying gig.

"Nancy, we are thrilled to be on the ground floor of such an exciting idea," Brenda says. "Right girls?"

"Absolutely. We are one hundred percent behind you. What a way to celebrate our love for Nancy Drew. I can't wait to see who you have for speakers," Marlene adds.

"I think you'll be impressed," I say, giving them all a big smile.

Yes, my trusty old big fake smile. And girls if you only knew —I can't wait to see who I will have for speakers too!

CHAPTER TWO

*I*t's wrong. I'm not a sociopath; I get it. Sometimes in life, you have to do what you have to do. That's what I keep telling myself, anyway. And he was so stubborn about it. All he had to do was co-sign and I wouldn't have had to go to these lengths. It could have been a normal loan. If he had shown his true colors before we were married, there wouldn't have been a wedding. But now I'm trapped. What's the old Ann Landers question? Are you better off with him or without him? I'm too old to start over. I was so lonely when we met. Mr. Charming painted a picture of us living on Mackinac Island and growing old together in total bliss. He failed to mention what a grouch he can be to me. The rest of the island knows him as friendly, cheerful, and easy-going. That's what I thought too, until the honeymoon was over. I was doing fine in Traverse City after my divorce from my first husband. I should have stayed single. But my money was running out. The thought of getting a steady minimum wage job again, ugh. And there he was. I had no idea agreeing to work at a booth at the forestry convention was going to change my life.

Accepting that invitation for coffee … if only I had said no. Who can resist coffee and dimples? His story was intriguing, and he seemed so kind and sure of himself. First, early retirement from a forestry career and then moving to the house he inherited from his grandparents on Mackinac Island. He couldn't wait to focus on his passion for woodworking and carving. He was lonely too, once his wife passed. His attentiveness to my awful divorce story touched my heart. Saying "sparks flew" was putting it mildly. In hindsight, our hormones took over our better judgement. We hardly knew each other. Who gets married after only three months of dating? Stupid! So stupid.

Here we are ... almost two years in and all the truth has revealed itself. I married a miserly, grouchy, stingy man who spends all his time woodworking and ignoring me. If we could have an honest conversation, something we aren't capable of without a fight, he would say he feels as betrayed as I do as to what he thought he was getting in a wife. The attentive, adoring, agreeable woman he dated was not being honest either. Piper will never know how she saved my life with her little shop and art classes. This little spot on the map of a tiny island, so aptly named The Creative Lilac, has become one of my favorite places in the entire world. As long as she doesn't push the whole religion thing on me, she has such a calming presence. She doesn't. She could come off as some kind of "preachy girl." I don't think she can help herself. She simply *likes* God, or Jesus, or whatever it is that's tripping her trigger. I don't get it, but it seems to mean everything to her. I can't blame her for wanting to talk about it, or him ... or whatever that whole thing is.

"Oh, hey. I didn't expect you home so soon. I wasn't sure if you were cooking dinner, so I'm making myself a sandwich," Ned says as I lock the door behind me.

"Things went well at our meeting. We are in the planning stages of the convention, so there's a lot to do," I say, avoiding the fact that I thought I made it clear he didn't marry Betty Crocker. I'm *not* the cook in this house. Obviously, wifey number one played that role to a tee. Hello, Martha Stewart.

"I was surprised it was going ahead after the whole loan

thing. I can tell you're still mad I wouldn't co-sign," he says, putting too much mustard on his bread.

"I told you, don't worry about it. Some of the other people were able to come up with the initial funds, but they still want me to run everything, so it all worked out," I say.

"I can't put this property at risk. You knew before we were married that my pension and anything I have will be going to my kids. I get that seems odd to you when they both live in foreign countries and barely see me, but as a dad, it's what I need to do," he says, finally noticing the excess mustard and wiping it off. "It's what Leslie would have wanted."

Every time he mentions his wife's name, he whispers it, like she's a ghost standing in the room watching his every move. More than a ghost, she's often the elephant in the room as far as I'm concerned. Listen, bub. I'm no Leslie, and I never will be.

"Leslie has moved on, but it's your money to do with what you will. There really wasn't risk because it's going to be a success. If anything, it would have made money. Like I said, I'm running the convention, not funding it—so don't worry about it," I say.

"I wouldn't if you wouldn't walk around with a chip on your shoulder. I know we're in a rough patch. This seems to be the thing you won't let go when it comes to me," he says. "Cam and Piper Nelson are a young couple with a store to keep up. Cam is always busy at the Grand. He is an excellent groundskeeper from the conversations I've had with him. I can't believe they would risk what they have built for a convention."

Bite your tongue, Nancy. If you walk into this trap, it will only get worse. Thank you, Nancy Drew, for the lesson you taught me in *The Secret of the Old Clock*—always stifle a snarky comeback, and don't let anyone get the best of you.

"Like I said, I'm into the planning of the event. I'm not even sure who figured it out, but they did. And we were tasked with keeping everything private, sticking to our jobs, and not worrying about the funding. So that's what I'm doing. I'm terribly busy with lots of details. I'm sure no one wants people asking questions about their private financial affairs," I say.

That should shut him up and stop his wondering about the money.

"Look at it this way—you can give all your attention to your woodworking," I say, mustering the lightest tone I can.

"Whatever."

And with that charming statement, there he goes to his heated woodworking garage—an expense that didn't seem to fit into his grand plan of leaving everything to his children when it benefited him. At least I got the little cove room looking out over the lake for my personal space. When I shut the door, I pretend this is my place, only my place. Hopefully, he'll get involved in a project and forget all about the convention and the details. I think I covered all my bases with the girls and him. I'm glad he brought up Cam, because I know they have coffee occasionally. The last thing I need is him piquing Cam's interest to start questioning Piper. No one needs to know the truth about how I'm getting this done. Now if I can keep all these plates spinning ... and my stories straight.

If.

CHAPTER THREE

MARCH 1983

*I*t's not advertised in the travel brochures, but for those of us who live here all year, the winter can be very long. I'm not going to waste today's glimpse at spring. Anyway, I need a breather. The unseasonable anticipated forty-five degrees is a big deal and everyone is in a good mood ... even Ned. Waking up to coffee and a warm bagel from him is not his norm. Every once in a while, I see the guy who courted me, the one I thought I was marrying. But then he grumbles about something, and I'm gone again in my heart.

Ahhh ... there's the Grand ... so quiet and peaceful before the crowds descend in a few months. The girls went crazy when I told them our committee will be allowed to stay overnight during the convention and have all the same meals provided to the attendees. It feels good to give them some perks, as they are working so hard.

Piper was super excited that I was able to get the okay for Sister Mary Margaret to share her room. She has brought me so much joy since I met her, it feels good to be able to give something back that makes her happy. Truth is, they will be so busy, they won't get the real Grand pampering that every guest gets.

No spending all the idle time on one of the world's longest porches, rocking away the moments in a wicker chair.

I know Piper stayed there when she first landed on the island a while back, but for the other ladies, it will be the first time. Piper even said that living in their cottage next door, just off the corner of the porch, hasn't dampened the wonder of the place. I get that. Looking at the Straits of Mackinac, the bridge, how the water changes color as Lake Michigan meets Lake Huron ... it's not something I ever want to take for granted. Sometimes I even think it's worth having married Ned to get to live here. Sometimes.

"Look at you. You're off in la-la land somewhere!"

Oh, no. I should have noticed the swishing skirt sound heading my way. What is she doing so far from her Main Street lair?

"Hello, Katherine. I'm surprised to see you so far from your office in this chilly weather. Aren't you cold in your skirt ... with ... are those roses on the fabric and on your shoes? Aren't you afraid of slipping?" I ask. "There are still little patches of ice after all."

"My goodness, Nancy. Your concern for my well-being is touching. You don't know your island flowers, do you? Of course, you're not from here, not one of the originals, so why would you? One step short of a 'fudgie,' still, am I right?"

Ugh. Katherine Sims-Dubois, the illustrious town chair-woman. The town snob, busy-body, husband leering, fake who has made it her business since I arrived to let me know I don't fit in. Islanders don't use the term "fudgie" with affection. I live here year-round, lady. She's so snarky.

The one group she hasn't won over is Piper and her friends. I've heard through the grapevine The Creative Lilac is the one property she can't get her hands on. If she does, she'll basically own the whole town and make everyone her puppets.

"Do enlighten me, Katherine. If those flowers aren't some type of rose, what are they?"

"Why, only one of the islands premiere spring flowers which will be popping up around here in the not-to-distant future, after wintah. They are lady slippers. They were my motha's favorite."

There it is … that goofy sound of her dialect which made no sense to me until Piper clued me in on the British-American hybrid style of speaking used in the earlier 1900s called the Transatlantic dialect. This Katherine thinks she's Katherine Hepburn or something!

Piper said it's because she spent a brief time at an English boarding school, which is ridiculous, since most of her life was spent right here where no one else speaks that way. So pretentious. One of the first things she said when I met her made my eyes roll back in my head. *"Notice there are no caaahs on the island."* Those softer vowels, dropping r's and emphasizing t's hit the last nerve in my spine to hear her say *wintah* instead of winter.

Even Ned's mother has mentioned she's a big fraud. Hmmmm, takes one to know one.

"Surely, you've seen the lady slippers blooming in the spring?" she says with an over-the-top hand-gesture.

Please. That over-dyed black beehive hairdo, her long pink nails, and infamous swishy skirts—what a joke. She always has something outlandish on the hems and on the tips of her pumps. Yeah, you are something, but I wouldn't say "lady." Someone should blow her "covah" because she is a phony beyond compare. Remember the lesson from *The Hidden Staircase*, Nancy. *If you're around a gossip, you better put up your guard and be extra sneaky!*

"How long have you been here now? Two years, is it? And how is that gorgeous husband of yours?" Katherine asks.

"Ned is doing fine."

"You know, we had coffee a few times when he was tending to the paperwork regarding his grandparents' house. I always found him quite charming. I remember hearing about his plans to retire soon and I thought we might become fast friends when he settled here, but then, here he comes with a new bride. A bit shocking really. How long *did* you date?" Katherine asks.

"Long enough to have him ask me to marry him, even though he had met you. Funny, huh?"

"Yes, and now I understand you have scuttled together some sort of convention this fall at the Grand. A Nancy Drew convention, I believe," she says with one painted-on eyebrow raised.

"I'm part of the group bringing it here. It will bring some new people to the island, which is always good for tourism."

"Who did you say is funding this mystery convention?"

"I didn't. I'm working on the committee, and that's where I'm putting my efforts. Organization is what I'm good at."

"Yes, shocking to hear about the quick cancellation of the original convention that weekend, but then, the island will not tolerate scandalous headlines. I won't hear of it. You may have noticed I always know what's going on. I make it my business. I mean, England has the queen, and the island has …. well, my undying loyalty," she says.

Really? You now think you are the queen of Mackinac Island? Oh, great. She's still talking.

"Nothing, and I mean nothing gets past me. I've made it my business to understand more about this little soiree you're putting together. I read some of those books growing up. I'm a bit of a Nancy Drew aficionado myself. I particularly enjoyed— I believe it was the eighth volume—*Nancy's Mysterious Letter.* One of the times the villain in the story got away. Wasn't that delicious?"

"Interesting. Out of all the stories, you can relate to the villain," I say, raising *my* eyebrow.

"Aren't you precious? If you need a speaker, I might make myself available."

"We're good."

"Oh. Well. Your loss."

I can see it's taking her a minute to recover from someone saying "no" to her majesty.

"Still hanging out with Piper and her gaggle? I suppose they will be helping?"

"Oh, look at the time." I say, pushing back my sleeve to reveal there is no watch.

"Of course, I'll be in attendance along with some of the other important island ladies. I introduce myself at all the conventions. By then, I'll have uncovered all the juicy details of how you pulled off a major convention with your meager background. Now that's a mystery that maybe even Nancy Drew couldn't solve, but I will," she says.

She's back in "full Katherine" mode.

"Anyhoo, it's nice to get a breather from the long wintah. Oh, and say hello to dahling Ned for me. What a gorgeous man. With those dimples he has a distinct resemblance to Clark Gable. I've been told I look like Vivien Leigh. Wouldn't we have been a pair in *Gone With the Wind*? Do remind him I'm always available for a chat and a cup of tea, won't you? Maybe when you're busy at one of your convention meetings, we'll get together. We wouldn't want poor Ned to get lonely, now, would we? Tah!"

And swish, swish, swish …. off she goes. She thinks she's so "clevah." I hope she falls and breaks her hip! I still have no idea what she was doing in this quiet part of town at this time of year. It's almost like she was stalking me. Maybe it's time for me to do some stalking of my own.

CHAPTER FOUR

"*He*'s not going to know, Penny, I told you. Just keep your end of the agreement, and it will all be fine. Only you and I know. As far as anyone else is concerned, it was totally normal," I say trying to sound as persuasive as anyone can on a phone call. "Listen, he's going to be home soon, and I can't be overheard having this conversation with you. Transfer the payment. They are expecting it. We're getting a lot of interest in the convention. Trust me, it's all good. Angel investors were the way to go. Don't be worried."

"Worried about what?" Ned asks.

Why didn't I hear him come in? I should put a bell on that guy.

"Listen, I need to go. Don't worry about anything *Susie*. My husband is home, so we'll talk again soon," I say, gently hanging up the phone and trying to nonchalantly wipe the sweat off my palms.

"Susie?" he asks.

"Someone I've met, another Nancy Drew fan. She's concerned about some of the details, and I had to set her straight. It's all good. Like I told her, nothing to worry about," I say.

Gosh, I'm getting so good at lying.

"Did you just come in? I didn't hear you. I could have opened the door for you," I say.

"I heard you say something about worry as I was opening the door. I wanted to know if you needed help or something," he says, putting some groceries in the cupboard.

"No. Everything's fine. Some of these people aren't used to conventions, so I have to explain how it will work," I say.

"I'm still confused about how it all got funded. Originally, you said you needed the collateral of this place, or it wouldn't be possible. I'm interested in—"

"Ned! I told you. Other people handled it. You aren't on the committee, and it's really not your concern. The minute you chose not to co-sign the loan, you chose not to be involved. It's not something you need to think about," I say, raising my voice.

"But you are my concern, and you are involved. If something goes south, can you be sued? That would affect me … marital property laws and all …"

"It doesn't sound like concern for me at all. It sounds like a concern once again for you and your money. Let's just say what it is: you love your money more than you love me," I say. "We can't talk about this without you showing your true colors to me, and your true colors are green, money green."

"Nancy, it's not true. I couldn't help you with that risky of a proposition. If you needed money for your health or something like that, I would give you everything," he says.

"That means you get to decide what is important to me. You should have said yes because I asked. That should have been enough. I already told you; it's handled. None of it is your concern. Can we please never talk about it again, and can you please not bug other people about it? Can you at least do that and respect my wishes?"

"Fine! I won't bring it up again. It's clear I can't talk to you about something that has taken over your life. I'm not supposed to have an opinion. Do I have it right?"

"Yes, you have it right," I say.

"Fine!" And there he goes, slamming the door on his way out.

At least he didn't hear my whole conversation with Penny. She owed me one and she knows it. That's why I got her to set up the angel investor loan where she works. She put in the paperwork with the two required signatures. Only she and I know I signed both my and Ned's name. I couldn't get the loan without his signature too. With that thorough background check, there wouldn't be a loan without his collateral. If Penny keeps her mouth shut and doesn't panic, it will work out. If everyone just does what they're told, it will all be fine.

Knock, knock.

Why do I jump from a simple knock on the door?

Knock, knock.

Why is Ned knocking … is he trying to make some kind of point?

Knock, knock.

Ned, as soon as I open this door, you are getting another earful.

"Oh. Hi, Cam. I thought maybe you were Ned. Piper's not here. We had our meeting at her studio," I say.

"Hi, Nancy. No, actually I was looking for Ned. I ran into him at the grocery store, and he was telling me about his latest woodworking project. He said I should stop by and see it. Is he out in his area?" Cam asks.

"Yes, he's out there, I'm sure."

"You guys have all been so busy with the convention getting closer. It's all Piper can talk about! She's beyond excited and even showed me the brochure and poster ideas she's come up with. You know Piper. She loves to tell me everything!" Cam says. "Well, thanks, Nancy. I'll go find Ned …"

I have never known a guy with such vibrant red hair. It compliments Piper's blonde hair and somehow their eyes both match the unique blue water that surrounds the bridge across the Straits. Wait, what did he just say?

"Hold up, Cam. You said Piper tells you everything?"

"Down to the last detail. I think it's her love language. I had to learn how to be a much better listener. If it's obvious I missed out on something she said because I wasn't paying attention, she is not too happy," he says with a wink.

"So, you talk about the convention?" I ask.

What was that wink for? Does he know about me funding everything?

"Every night at dinner. She loves telling me about it. Well, I'll pop into Ned's shop. Don't work too hard. I know most of this is on your shoulders," Cam says, closing the door.

Piper, if you said something to him about me handling the finances, and he says something to Ned…I'm going to kill you! What am I going to do with her? It's just like when Nancy has problems with Bess and George in *The Sign of the Twisted Candles*. You people. Can't you all just shut up!

CHAPTER FIVE

"Freddy, is Piper available? I really need to speak with her," I say as I close the door.

Normally I love the gentle tinkling bell of welcome from the door at The Creative Lilac, but like everything else lately, it feels like one more thing to irritate me. There's the gatekeeper Freddy. But him, I like. I was touched after first meeting him when Piper clued me in on how important he is to her and Cam, even though they aren't related. He was her neighbor when she lived out west. When she married Cam, they brought him here to live near them. He seems to be her "right-hand man" in the store.

Who doesn't love a friendly greeting from an elderly, pseudo-uncle type when you're out of sorts? Ever since he got a pun-a-day calendar for Christmas, it's impossible to get past him without hearing a joke. Maybe that will help my mood.

"Oh, Mrs. Nancy, I'm not sure what she's doing upstairs, but I'll hit the intercom for you. But, before I do, you have to hear this one! Yesterday, I sent my girlfriend a huge pile of snow. I called her up today, and asked, 'Did you get my drift?'"

And here comes his laughter, which normally is far funnier than the joke he feels he has to share.

"Get it, get *my drift?*" More laughter.

"You have become quite the stand-up comic, Freddy. I'm kind of in a hurry. Can you see if Piper can see me for a minute?" I ask.

Someone is probably regretting giving Freddy that calendar.

"You bet. I couldn't resist telling you that good joke. We all need a good joke every day, don't you think? Pip, Mrs. Nancy is here to see you," Freddy says over the intercom.

"Wonderful, send her on up!"

"One more, Mrs. Nancy! What do you get when you cross a bell and a hummingbird?" Freddy asks.

"Freddy, I think Piper is waiting for me ..."

"A humdinger! Get it? A humdinger! That's a good one. Have a nice meeting," he says as I'm halfway up the stairs.

I can still hear him giggling. The man does love his own jokes.

"Hey, Nancy, nice to see you!" Piper says, gesturing to have a seat by her at the big table in her workspace. "I'm surprised you have time to stop by, but I'm always glad to see you."

"I'm sorry to drop in, but something is bothering me. I need to get it cleared up," I say.

"Oh? What's on your mind?"

"Did you tell Cam about the financial part of the convention? Did you tell him anything about how I'm handling it?" I ask.

"No, I didn't. You said not to, and I respect that. He asked about the finances in passing, but I told him it's all internal business."

"So, you didn't say anything other than that?"

"No, Nancy, I didn't. Why do you think I did?"

"Cam stopped over to see Ned's latest project and he mentioned how excited you were about the convention, and how you tell him everything."

"Yes, everything I'm *allowed* to tell him, but nothing more. He didn't ask any further once I told him it was internal business. I don't think he cares that much about the details, but he knows I care if *he* is paying attention to what's important to me. I try to do the same for him. You seem really rattled by this. Is there something going on?"

"No. Well, not really. It's just that I need to know if I can trust you and the girls on the committee. When I say to keep something private, I want it that way, even with spouses."

"I mean, I get it. You made that really clear in the meeting, and I believe we all took you seriously. Are you afraid someone is gossiping about the convention or something?" she asks.

"I'm overreacting, as usual. I ran into Katherine, and she was asking all kinds of nosy questions and inferring things like she always does, and I guess it set me on edge," I say.

"I can't figure out why she does that to everyone. She could be doing so much good in her position, but she likes to cause trouble. I really try to steer clear of her. It's better that way because I can't seem to have an authentic conversation with her. That grudge over me not selling this place when I first got to town never goes away. I think The Creative Lilac brings something unique to the island. As the town chairwoman, that should make her happy. But, instead, she always seems angry when I'm around."

"She let me know she plans on making some kind of appearance to welcome the attendees and that she is, in fact, a Nancy Drew fan herself. She offered to be a speaker. I shut that down very fast. As much as I'm not crazy about having her and her minions there, it will be more registrants for the convention. We'll take all of those we can get."

"You're right. She'll try to steal the show. It's not anything we haven't seen before. At least we are prepared for it. We can all do our best to make sure she doesn't disrupt any of the activities. We'll be prepared and keep an eye on her," Piper says.

"I hope I didn't come down too hard on all of you at our meetings. I didn't want to have to ask about not talking about God, but it's not the time or place."

"I'm happy you made it clear because if you hadn't, I probably would have done just that. When I know my boundaries, I respect the rules. You don't have to worry about me or any of the girls. We're pretty trustworthy."

"Can I be totally honest with you?"

"Yes, I prefer it,"

"Why *do* you always bring the conversation around to religion? I mean, everyone has their own beliefs. Unless someone specifically asks you about yours, why do you bring it up? It can make people feel pretty uncomfortable. People have priests, pastors, rabbis, and there's always Billy Graham on TV ..."

I can't believe I brought this up, but I'm genuinely curious.

"Can I be totally honest *with you?*" she asks.

Finally, I'm going to see the "real" Piper.

"The Piper you know is a relatively new person on the planet. You didn't know 'the Piper' who grew up with a hypocritical father who was right up there with Billy Graham in notoriety on California TV. Only one problem—his words didn't match how he lived or treated his family," she says, looking off in the distance.

"I know your family passed, but I didn't know that part of it ..."

"It is a very sad thing for me, but what's just as sad are the years I wasted walking around thinking I knew who Jesus was, and what being a Christian was. I treated it like an insurance plan or a 'get out of Hell free' card. Not going to Hell? Check! I still went through life with its highs and lows, getting by. But I missed the big picture, of why Jesus did all He did on the cross, and how it affects the life I am called to live while I'm here. When I see people walking around, oblivious to all God has for them right now, not only in Heaven, I speak up," Piper says.

"You really do speak up," I say with a smile.

"You noticed, huh?"

There's no irritation in her voice. I expected her to act offended.

"Imagine if your car broke down, and you were stranded along the side of a road. I drive by and wave. I see your predicament, but I don't stop. I don't tell you there are mechanics in town who can help you; I simply leave you there. What would you think of me?" Piper asks.

"I guess I would think you're a jerk! You had a way to help me, and you didn't," I say quietly.

"You get the picture. Nancy, there are so many privileges being a child of God. There's peace, hope, strength ... His guiding and guarding. The best one of all—to finally be done, or at least be better at being done with a life of 'me, me, me.' Being self-absorbed led me to feeling bitter, angry, and for me ... depression," she says.

"You? Depressed? I can't imagine that."

"Without staying close to Jesus, I would be depressed. Yes, He rescued me from Hell, but He also gives me a thriving, crazy good life here on Earth that has nothing to do with money, or never having problems. It has everything to do with peace no matter what comes along. And the stuff always comes along, for everyone," she says.

"I can agree with you on that," I say.

"That's a part of living in a fallen world. This isn't Heaven. But this is the place where He asked us to tell other people about Him so they can have all He offers. We still have free will to choose to believe what He said or not. That's why, mostly without my planning it, my conversations usually lead to asking if someone knows Jesus," she says.

She does seem authentic and not someone who operates with a bad motive.

"Truth be told, if you didn't make it clear we shouldn't talk about being a believer at the convention, I probably would have. I totally respect your reasons and understand what you are saying. Thank you for making your expectations clear. It is *your* gig!" she says with a big smile.

"I mean ... I can see it's the right thing for you, but there are many religions and paths," I say.

What's up with me that I don't just let this go?

"Jesus knew we would all be introduced to lots of paths, and we could think that way. He said in John: I am the way and the truth and the life. No one comes to the Father except through me.' Nancy, have you ever read the Bible?"

"Read it, like sat down and read it for myself outside of hearing a preacher? Uh, no. It sounds like ... well ...over my head. I'm a fan of inspirational sayings here and there ...."

"Here," she says, picking up a book in a stack on the table. "Take this. It's the New Testament in modern language without all the 'thees and thous.' Start by reading the book of John. That's how I tell people to begin if they don't know where to start. Don't pre-judge. Read it with an open mind. See what happens."

"Well, thank you. You know how busy I am with the convention; it won't be at the top of my to-do list ... maybe after it's over and life settles down."

"I hear you. You have a lot to do, and if I can help more, please let me know. It's no coincidence you popped in today," she says. "I'm praying for the convention, and everyone involved. Don't worry, we all have your back, including helping with the 'town spokesperson.' She's someone I pray for a lot!"

"See, the whole praying for someone who works hard every day to make your life miserable, that's hard to swallow. You should be thinking up ways to get her back because that's what she deserves!"

"Here's the thing ... if I got what *I* truly deserved...it wouldn't be pretty. Jesus knows what I should have received, but He chose to love me and die for me anyway. So, if that's my benchmark, how can I do less for someone else? Do I get mad at first and plot some ways in my head to get back at her? Yes, yes, I do."

Oh, good. She is human.

"Then, I have to realize that isn't the way I'm called to live. I say I'm sorry and get back to forgiveness, which is a cornerstone of this whole new way of living. That's where the peace is. It's a renewing of my mind every day to be more like Him," Piper says. "God's got me, and God has every situation I face. *His* justice always wins in the end."

"You're a better person than I am. Listen, I've taken up enough of your time, and thanks for the talk. I'm not on your path, but I do appreciate being able to have an honest conversation. Those are few and far between for me these days," I say.

"I'm glad you feel you can be real with me. You know, Cam is enjoying getting to know Ned. I think he secretly wants to get into woodworking. The four of us should get together for something fun," Piper says, walking me down the stairs.

"Yes, when things quiet down," I say politely, but I have no intention of us hanging out. Piper, yes. Ned, no thanks.

Quickly sneaking out the door before Freddy can hit me with another joke while tucking the Bible in my bag, I'm thankful I brought my large satchel. The last thing I need is for some Bible thumper taking notice and inviting me to a church.

And there *she* is, standing on the sidewalk stroking some man's arm, swishing her skirt, flirting and ... wait! I recognize the back of that head and that plaid shirt. That's Ned!

CHAPTER SIX

I see them, Ned and Katherine, but they don't see me.
Do I try to get closer, hide if I can, and listen to their conversation—or do I walk right up to them, and let them know I see what's happening? Hmmm. Those boxes piled up in front of the store would be perfect to hide behind. A few more steps and, yes, there. They still can't see me, but I think I can hear them. Quiet down, tourists! I'm trying to hear.

"Then was that time you stopped in for tea, you know, before you were so occupied with other things in life. I think about that visit often, quite fondly actually," Katherine says, batting her eyes. "I think we're due for another visit, don't you? You can never have enough friends, and after all, we islanders have to stick together so we don't get overtaken by the fudgies."

More arm touching and I'm sure that last dig was meant for me. I wish one of her big false eyelashes would fall off right now. She's such a fake. Ned, wake up. Don't you get it?

"That was very kind of you to invite me for tea, Katherine. And it's been nice visiting, but I must get going. I have a few more stops, and as I was telling you, I need to get back to those projects waiting for me in my shop," Ned says.

What was that? He didn't really say no. And, oh, none of the grumpiness in his voice that I get to hear every day. Don't you make a cute couple. Long time islanders who could stick together and make beautiful music together. Now, that's precious.

"The invitation is always there if you get a minute. Tea for two, you know! Tah, Ned," Katherine says as Ned crosses the street and heads in the opposite direction.

Oh, man. Should I stay here until she's gone, or pop up right now and get in her face?

Swish. Swish. Swish. It's now or never.

"Oh! Nancy. You startled me. Where did you come from?" Katherine asks.

Good. She looks frazzled.

"I just dropped something and found it. Did I startle you?" I ask.

"Why, not at all. I hope you found what you were looking for," she says, obviously grappling to regain her usual arrogant composure.

"It's amazing what you can find here among the hustle and the bustle," I say.

Not sure if that made sense, but it's hard to think right now.

"Imagine running into you again. I suppose you're in this neck of the woods having a meeting with your troop about the convention. Would I be right about that?"

"No, you would be wrong. I just had some errands to run."

Hmmm … she's not going to even mention that she was just talking to my husband.

"Why haven't you invited *me* for tea, Katherine? I hear you have people over to chat," I say, glaring directly into her eyes.

Ah, good. She looks flustered again.

"Well, yes, I do, but purely for business meetings. Since we have no business to discuss, I'll have to pass. I must get to a meeting right now. Tah!"

Swish, swish, swish and off she goes.

Perfect! She now knows I saw her talking to my husband. Busted. Speaking of busted, can I count on Ned to tell me he ran into her? He has no business with her. Is she trying to start something with him? Would I care if she did?

CHAPTER SEVEN

alking back to our house, all I can think about is how much I can't stand Katherine and how much she and Ned deserve each other. Two conniving fakes that would be a perfect match. And why did I have to talk to Piper about God? That's one more thing I *don't* need to be thinking about.

What I *would* like to do is disappear into that wonderful world of River Heights so the *other* Nancy would deal with them all for me. *That* Nancy is brave, strong, and has the best friends! Bess and George were great buddies, and Nancy never even kissed Ned. Aw, a simple life as it should be. If I could take the scenery of Mackinac Island and combine it with the people in River Heights in all my favorite Nancy Drew books—now that's where I would like to be.

And here I am, back at my front door—my real world.

"Oh hi! I didn't know you were out. I went on a hunt for you when I got home, but you were nowhere to be found. Did you have a committee meeting today?" Ned asks as I close the door and drop my bag on the corner table near the door.

I think he knows I did.

"No, I just wanted to check in with Piper on a few things, so

I popped into The Creative Lilac. I was interested in some upcoming classes," I say, hoping I come off nonchalant.

"Classes? When would you have time for classes with all you have going on?" Ned asks.

"You're right. So, you were out too. Where did you go?"

"I had to hit the hardware store for a few hinges for that cabinet I'm making. So many tourists, though. It's hard to navigate the streets. I do run into a local once in a while."

"Oh? Anyone I know?"

"No, just a few pals from the marina. Boat talk, mostly. I think I'll build a boat at some point. That would be fun," he says.

"Yeah."

My heart is sinking. Something must be going on between them. Not one mention of seeing her.

"Should I grill some burgers? I'm getting hungry. Have you eaten?" he asks.

"I seem to have lost my appetite. You go ahead."

Even if I don't want him, I don't want her to have the satisfaction of being with him!

"Can you imagine you and me, out in the Straits in a boat I built? Now that would be something. We'd head on over to Round Island Lighthouse and reenact a scene from that movie they shot here you like so much. What was it? Somewhere on an Island?" Ned asks.

"It's *Somewhere in Time*. It's about true love, loyalty, and people who can trust each other."

"Yeah, that's it. *Somewhere in Time*. Did you know Cam and Piper were extras in that movie? Cam told me."

"Piper has mentioned it. That's right before they got married," I say, staring out the window.

I don't know why I'm bothering to keep talking to him other than the fact he's far less grumpy than normal. And no wonder. He's just had a rendezvous to set up a tea with the love of his life!

"I sure do like Cam. What a great guy. Even though he's younger, we can really relate," Ned says, taking the burgers out of the fridge and adding salt and pepper. "I like Piper too. She must be a good person to have on your committee."

"She is. Does Cam ever talk to you about, you know, spiritual things? God and stuff?"

Since this may be the last time I talk to Ned in a very long time, I'm wondering if Cam is as much of a religious nut as Piper is.

"Yeah, he does. But I don't mind it. He's not pushy. It's more like explaining why it's important to him and a part of his life," he says, slicing some buns and getting the condiments out of the fridge. "I think about what he says. I don't know. Maybe he's right. Maybe there is a God who loves us. Could be. What do I know?"

You should be listening to him, Ned, so you can see what a cheat you are! And how you're probably breaking commandments all over the place.

"Well, I'm ..." I start to say, but he's talking at the same time. I just want to get away from him.

"Oh, sorry. Didn't mean to talk over you. I did see someone else downtown. Katherine Sims-Dubois. She thinks because we had a cup of tea or coffee ... I hardly remember It ... that we are friends or something. She's a trip," he says.

He did tell me! Could it be that it doesn't mean anything or is he covering it up in case I'm on to him? I wish I knew my husband well enough to be sure.

"What were you going to say?" he asks.

"Maybe I will have a burger if you don't mind throwing one on for me, too."

"No problem. The more the merrier on the grill. I'll be back in a jiff with perfectly done burgers," he says, brushing past me and landing a kiss on my cheek.

Watching him head out the door, I'm not sure. Can I trust this man?

CHAPTER EIGHT

MAY 1983

"My most romantic island stop? Let's see. Hubby rented a carriage, and we did a moonlight ride past Sugarloaf, Arch Rock, British Landing ... it was wonderful. There was a full moon that night and everything glowed. He was so thoughtful, and it was romantic," Marlene said.

Someone thought "the most romantic island spots" was a good topic of conversation while we wait for Piper to handle some kind of urgent art question downstairs in the store. Wouldn't be my topic of choice!

"He was so thoughtful, and it *was* romantic," Marlene says with a sigh.

All the girls also give a sigh.

Please people. Don't you know romance is in books and fairy tales? Or maybe watch *Love Boat* but quit expecting it in real life. Even the island's beauty can't keep it alive once you say "I do."

"How about you and Ned, Nancy? Where is your most romantic spot on the island?" Gail asks.

"Sorry, ladies," Piper says, stepping back into the meeting. "Freddy didn't know which paint to recommend to a rather demanding customer, so I had to take care of that one. Where were we?"

"We were about to stay on track and dive into the details of why we are here ... the convention. Let's review," I say.

Whew. Glad I dodged that question of romance. I have no answer. Dating? Maybe. Marriage is a romance killer. Once the guy has got you, he reverts to not trying at all.

"Let's see. Registration packets are out to the Nancy Drew clubs across the country. Check. Piper, the artwork on the brochures is beautiful ... very 'Nancy-like' for sure. Check. Marlene, how many registrants do we have so far?" I ask.

"Well, we're a few months out from final registration, but so far we have hit the one-hundred mark!" Marlene says.

After waiting for the appropriate amount of hooting and hollering from this enthusiastic bunch, I need to get them back into order.

"Fantastic! We can handle only ninety more pre-registrations and we've reached our capacity. We do need to reach that number to be financially sound, but it looks very feasible. I'm also accounting for ten to twenty last-minute registrations, or even a walk-in or two. Okay, Brenda, catch us up on the Nancy Drew display," I say.

"I have a specific area set aside in the Grand Ballroom to display all the books we could gather. I tried to do some research on getting some first editions or something, but I abandoned that idea with the new budget numbers you gave me," Brenda explains.

"Good call. We have bigger fish to fry, so it's okay. I don't think first editions will be a big deal to the attendees," I say.

Darn! I was hoping we would have some kind of treasure to display, but I have to stick to what we can afford. Besides, what do I know about collectible books? I just loved reading Nancy Drew.

"Then, we've sent away to have Piper's artwork enlarged into hanging banners, which we will put all along the back wall. It will help create a special feeling when you walk in the door and see the magnificent ballroom totally adorned in Nancy Drew," Brenda says.

More clapping from the group.

"Sounds wonderful, Brenda. I think looking at the sketches you and Piper did of how they will turn out has given us all a clearer idea of what to expect. Excellent job. Now, Gail. How is speaker coordination coming?" I ask.

"Pretty good, I think. We got a librarian from Petosky, and one from Traverse City. The biggest 'get' is Maxwell D. Powers from lower Michigan. He's an expert on Nancy Drew. He's the name that kept coming up when I asked some clubs who we should get for speakers," Gail says. "His talk is called 'Sleuthing the Real Carolyn Keene.' Sounds like a good title to me."

"Good job! I don't know that much about him, but if the club people like him, that works for us," I say.

"And we've been able to stick to the plan of giving the attendees quality free time to explore the island. We're on track to have the welcome reception the first night and the mixer. This is a fun addition from when we last talked. Each welcome packet has a mystery quiz/scavenger hunt to be worked on throughout the weekend. Some helpers are lined up to wear sandwich board-style signs with clues about different books to help them with answers. Everyone who turns in a completed sheet of the correct answers at the end of the convention will be in a drawing for a Nancy Drew book of their choice," Gail says.

"I love that idea!" Marlene says.

"We had no trouble getting volunteers from the library club. Well, that and the church. I've been able to recruit quite a few helpers," Gail says. "The bookstore in Cheboygan is bringing a nice selection of used and new Nancy Drew books. They are giving us a twenty percent cut on their profits."

"That will be a big hit. I, for one, can't wait to hear from Maxwell Powers," Brenda says.

"We're lucky he lives in lower Michigan, or we could have

had a hefty flight bill. This isn't going to be any ordinary convention," I say.

They don't need to know Maxwell is the reason expenses have gotten a little out of hand. He didn't come cheap.

"Our last day will include a Nancy Drew art project, Nancy Drew bingo, and a fun Nancy Drew-themed tea party. It should be a one-of-a-kind experience. If I wasn't already involved, I would want to come, for sure!" Gail says.

"Fantastic job, Gail. And now Maxine ... hospitality?" I say.

"Yes, I've been coordinating with the Grand for our opening reception, the meals, the rooms, including arrivals, and luggage. Everything seems to be in order. Every person attending will receive a welcome packet with the layout of the weekend, maps of the Grand and the island, a fudge discount coupon, and various other discount coupons for island activities. I'm still working on things, but I feel like it's all coming together nicely. I'm pleased with the progress so far," Maxine says with an affirmative nod.

"Excellent, Maxine. I love your attention to detail. All of you, really. You've outdone yourselves. I couldn't have picked a finer group of ladies to work with," I say.

"Uh, there is one tiny thing I forgot to mention. We received a formal letter from the town chairwoman telling us she will be doing a welcoming speech on behalf of the island at the opening reception. *Telling*, mind you, not asking," Maxine says.

"In the spirit of 'choose your battles,' I guess that is going to happen. I was already told in person she expected to say a few words ... from the horse's mouth as it were," I say.

Giggles abound.

"Come on girls. Kindness always wins," Piper says.

"Oh, come on Piper. You of all people know how horrible she is. No one walks around calling the devil a nice guy," Brenda says. "Just once, I'd like to throw a pie in her face or something," Brenda gestures a throw.

Her tone and comical expression gets everyone giggling.

"Like I said, we're choosing our battles. We may have to deal with her on another front, but this is an easy one to let pass. Besides, she'll probably encourage her minions to attend. That's money in our pockets," I say.

I'm happy to see Piper nod in agreement. She sure takes her faith seriously even when she's often the brunt of Katherine's antics. My gal Piper has real integrity. What a pain in the neck!

CHAPTER NINE

JUNE 1983

"*W*hy did you say yes without asking me?" I can't help but glare at him.

Ugh Ned! Why did you accept an invitation to spend the Fourth of July with Piper and Cam with no regard to the fact I may not want to go?

"Because we don't do anything together and you've said yourself, you like Piper. I like Cam. Why can't we accept a nice invitation? It's the Fourth of July and we haven't done anything fun this summer. What's the big deal?" he asks. "Besides, they've arranged a private carriage tour for all of us with one of their friends driving, a picnic dinner on the Grand grounds, and a magnificent view of the fireworks. We can't see them that well from our place. Are you opposed to fun?"

"I have so much going on, the conference is getting closer and —"

"So, no. You don't have a good excuse other than you don't want to be with me," he says.

It's too close to the conference to cause trouble with him.

"Fine. I'll go. Next time, could you just ask me first? I don't think that's an unreasonable request."

"I hear you. Message received. By the way, there's a packet

for you that came in the mail. It's on the stand by the door. Looks like it's from your old stomping ground," he says.

"Oh?"

Why is he so nosy, and why am I getting something from Traverse City? I hope it's nothing from Penny and the loan. No news is good news, probably.

"I'm looking forward to a fun Fourth. I'll see you later. I have to get going on my project in my shop. Enjoy your afternoon," he says heading for the door.

Good. Get out of my hair and give me the house to myself. I can hardly wait for the door to close. I hope there's not more trouble in that envelope. Ripping it open, it doesn't seem to be formal papers. Hmmmmm. Oh great. This has to be Phillip's doing. I'm dealing with one husband; I don't need more grief from my ex. Why is he sending me our old love letters from when we were dating? What's his point? This handwriting that used to make me smile now makes me feel like I'm in the middle of an Alfred Hitchcock movie. He's never been one to be nostalgic. There's usually an ulterior motive with everything he does. Maybe I'm overreacting. Could he just be cleaning out a closet and not want them anymore?

Looking closer at his letters all this time later, something that eluded me is now crystal clear. The subtle jabs, veiled threats, and his manipulation woven throughout each letter. I wish I knew then what I know now. I don't trust him one bit. This is some kind of effort to reopen old wounds and stir up trouble. He's looking for "old Nancy" to react the way I normally would, bowing down to his wishes. But those days are over. Maybe he's trying to reconnect because he needs money, and he thinks this will make me drop my guard.

I know what I'll do. Nothing. I'm not even sure how he got my address here; I don't remember passing it along. I guess it's not that hard to send something to the island.

He's messing with me, trying to get me to respond. Too bad,

Phillip. I read *The Spider Sapphire Mystery*. Letters didn't stop Nancy Drew from moving forward and they won't stop me.

Here I am, stuck in another rotten marriage. What kind of idiot am I? *That* will be the lessons of the letters. Quit making the same mistakes! He was a jerk, and he is a jerk.

Knock, knock.

"Nancy? It's Piper. Do you have a minute?"

"I'll be right there," I say shoving the letters back in the envelope and then into my bag laying on the chair by the table.

"Hi! Come on in. What's up?" I ask, painting on a fake smile.

"I wanted to drop off the new sketch for the welcome banner. I need to get it to the printer," she says. "It's been so crazy with the Lilac Festival this month. I'm always amazed by the number of tourists that come to see our beautiful purple gems and soak up their fragrance. It's great for sales, but not for my time. I'm happy to have these finished and ready to go."

"Yes, I try to avoid downtown if I can. It is fun to see their faces when they come upon a lilac tree. I'm enjoying every lovely bloom myself. Let's see. Nice use of colors! Oh, yes. It's perfect, good to go. I like how the pictures and copy seem to pop off the page. Thanks for bringing it by. I don't want to hold you up," I say handing back the sketch and hoping she leaves quickly.

"Are you okay? You look a little flushed," she says.

"I'm okay. I got some mail I wasn't expecting, and it, well, I don't know. It bothered me, I guess."

"Anything I can do?"

"No, it's fine. I'll be fine. So, I guess we will be spending the Fourth together. That will be fun," I say, trying to feign excitement.

It's not that these aren't perfectly lovely people who will make wonderful company ... it's that anytime the four of us are together, I run the risk of someone bringing up the finances. I'll have to declare a "no convention conversation" day. That will sound good to everyone and should keep me safe.

"You know I'm here for you if you need to talk," Piper says.

"Honestly, Piper, that's sweet. I admire you so much, but sometimes you're too perfect!"

Couldn't hold it in, could you Nancy? That makes her eyes pop.

"I'm not trying to insult you, but *I'm* a very flawed person. It feels like your religion comes easy to you. All that *goodness* makes me feel 'less than' when I'm around you. I don't mean that to sound harsh. You caught me at a bad time," I say.

Wow! I've even surprised myself at how blunt I can be. Here is the person giving her all for the Nancy Drew convention, and I'm insulting the very core of who she is. Good one, Nancy, although it backs up what I said. A *very* flawed person.

"Nancy!" Piper says with her mouth hanging open.

Oh, boy, here it comes. Now she's going to give it to me.

"I am so glad you told me this!" Piper says.

"What? You're supposed to be punching me in the mouth right about now. This is further proof that we aren't from the same tribe or something. I just can't live up to your standards. When I'm around you, I feel it all the more," I say, not looking at her.

Okay. I did not expect to hear a lighthearted belly laugh.

"I am so sorry that is how you see me! You think I'm some goody-two shoes with none of your same temptations and life is easy for me? I am giving you the wrong impression. Most days, I'm a mess. Anything going right with me is because I see it through the lens of the greatest love I will ever know."

"Cam? Yeah, that's the other thing. You two have the perfect marriage. He's attentive, caring, affectionate, and kind. The rest of us are hanging out here in the carnival's haunted house while the two of you are always in the tunnel of love."

"No, I don't mean Cam when I say the greatest love. The

greatest love story is Jesus adopting me into His forever family as His child."

Oh great. Now I've gone and done it. I opened the door for this conversation.

"Have you ever heard of color blindness?" she asks.

"Yeah, my dad had it. He couldn't see colors," I say.

"That's how it is to see the world through your own eyes before you ask Jesus into your heart. You think you are seeing the true colors of things, and it seems normal. If you ever were to see things through a special pair of glasses, or have your condition corrected, you'd be amazed by what you see ... how colorful things really are and what you've been missing. That's what it was like for me when I went from living for myself to living for Jesus. I didn't get it before, either. You know, like that moment in *The Wizard of Oz* when Dorothy steps out of her house into Oz and it changes to color. You are living in a black and white world, and it's doable. But you are missing out on all that's really there. You don't see it fully and abundantly like God planned from the beginning of time for you to see it. Does that make sense?"

"Makes *more* sense, anyway. Why do you want this so much, and I simply don't?" I ask.

"Accepting Jesus is done by faith, like how we felt when we were kids before life bombarded us and we ended up hurt and afraid to trust people. When we make the decision to follow Jesus, a miracle happens. He comes to live in our hearts, and so does the Holy Spirit who becomes our comforter and our guide. The fact we are in each other's life means He has put me in your life for a reason. Yes, because it's fun to work on the Nancy Drew Convention, but also for something even more important. Your soul—the essence of the real you. He wants you for His daughter ... not only so you'll spend eternity with Him when your time on Earth is through, but also to have a fantastic life with Him in the here and now," she says.

"I've always felt like God set up a bunch of rules, gave us all these desires and inclinations that don't match His, and then waits around for us to screw up so He can punish us," I say.

"That's how a lot of people see it, and it couldn't be further from the truth. It says in John—in that Bible I gave you—that God loved the world so much He sent His only Son, that whosoever believes in Him would not perish, but have eternal life. You and I are the 'whosoever.' God so loved Nancy and Piper that He gave His only son Jesus, that if Nancy and Piper would believe in Him, they would not perish but have everlasting life. That's why I want you to read that Bible when you get time. See, it's not about someone being preachy, or a good person... none of us can measure up to perfection. Jesus came as a baby to Earth as a human. Even though He was tempted just like we are, He never sinned. Instead, He took on every sin of every person who ever has or ever will live. When we die and go before God, He won't wonder what good things we did, because they can never measure up. But, if we've accepted the truth about Jesus, what God will see is our advocate, Jesus. His verdict will be 'not guilty' ... come on in and enjoy all that has been prepared for you in Heaven!" she says with a tear falling out of the corner of her eye.

"So, that's it ... tell Jesus I acknowledge what He did?" I ask.

"Yes, acknowledging that He did it for you. If you authentically are sorry for your sin and accept Him as your Lord from that point on, the Bible says you get your name written in the Lamb's Book of Life," she says.

"Like a literal book?" I ask.

"I think so, at least however books exist in Heaven. It's some type of system that has a notation of your decision to follow Jesus," she says.

"Then, poof, and life is perfect?" I ask.

That brings out a big giggle.

"Wouldn't that be nice—a perfect, easy life. In our humanness, that's what we would all choose. But actually, the Christian walk is called the 'narrow road' because it's hard. We are still battling our old flesh. The Bible says our enemy, the devil, prowls around like a roaring lion to see who he can devour. He hates us and doesn't want us following Jesus. So, the only way we get through all this is to stay close to the Father, the Son, and the Holy Spirit. We read our Bible, we pray, and we make sure to hang out with other Christians who encourage us. That's what church is about. We are always learning, growing, supporting each other, and fighting the good fight together," she says.

"Onward Christian soldiers, huh? Isn't that kind of like a cult?"

I'm not pulling any punches. I want to have a real conversation with someone for once.

"Oh, you know there are some people out there who really use the Bible to point to themselves as the savior. More devil deviation tactics. The Holy Spirit tells us to test what we hear, to hold it up against God's word to determine if it's from God or not. We don't get the answers to all of life's questions while we are here, but we are told we can have peace in any situation and circumstance because He walks with us through everything," she says. "That's one of those mysteries in a world filled with mystery."

"I think some people in town think you are a cult."

"I've heard that, even though it's not true. What is true is Christians still get sick, lose their jobs, have tough times … you see what I mean. This isn't Heaven, yet. Our rewards aren't short-term, they are big picture and forever," she says. "So, what about you? Do you want to trust Jesus right now?"

"Honestly, no. I do feel more interested, but also more confused. I'm glad to clear up those cult rumors. So, right now, is this my only chance?" I ask.

Is there a *Go to Heaven or Miss Out* game show? Ugh. Glad I didn't say that out loud.

"That's between you and God. The only thing I will say is, none of us know how long we're here. When we aren't here anymore, then it is too late. Give what we talked about some thought and talk to Jesus. Tell Him you're interested and pay attention to what happens next in your life," she says. "He won't let you down."

"You're still kind of preachy," I say with a wink.

"Ah, not the first time I heard that. Hey, if you were me, and knew you could tell everyone the greatest story ever told, what would you do?"

"Probably not waste your time with people like me," I say.

"I love your sense of humor. And it's not like I'm recruiting people for Jesus and trying to hit some kind of sales number or something. Not at all. My prayer is that I only speak out of love to people who Jesus has me meet. It's that simple," she says.

"Oh, so no new car or trip to Bermuda for you from reaching your quota? I wouldn't want to hold you back," I say, trying to lighten up the conversation. "So, I suppose you pray for me?"

"Oh, yes. I pray for you, your marriage, the convention ... all of it. Today is an answer to prayer. I didn't come over here to talk to you about this, but sometimes God just opens a door, and we walk through it," she says. "And you did seem upset when I came in."

"Okay, since you laid it all on the table, I might as well. I just got a packet of letters from my ex ... our old love letters. He's not a nice guy. I can assure you what might seem like a nice gesture to someone else is not from him. There's probably been enough time since our divorce that he wants to mess with me in some way," I say.

"Did he send a note or ask for something? Do you have any connection to him?"

"No, no note. No connection. He is evil. It was a nasty divorce. He accomplished what he set out to do: upset me. I'm going to ignore it. It's probably nothing, but he's still the jerk he once was. Oh, and I'm not mentioning this to Ned, so please don't say anything in front of him or Cam. And that's another thing, Piper. If we're going to be friends, it has to be you and me. I can't have you share anything we talk about with Cam. Is that a problem for you?"

"No. He's a typical guy and doesn't ask much. I'm the one with all the questions, usually."

"And when we get together on the Fourth, can you help me make it a 'no convention' talk day? How do I put this, so you don't take it wrong ... Ned and I aren't on the best terms. I don't need him delving into my personal things. I know that sounds weird, but that's the way it is. He sure does like Cam."

"Yes. We'll make it a no convention conversation day, and yes, I *can* keep anything you tell me between us," she says.

"I appreciate that. The convention is going well, but there still are a lot of details and pressures. Getting together on the Fourth will be a nice break. I need it. And I will think about what you told me. Not sure I will read the Bible, but hey, never say never, right?"

"Hey ladies! I didn't know you were here, Piper," Ned says.

We were so busy talking I didn't see him and Cam walk by the window to the door.

"Yes, she popped in to show me a sketch for the convention. Excellent work as usual," I say, hoping he doesn't clue into the seriousness of our conversation. I don't need him to ask any questions.

"Oh, Nancy, I forgot to tell you! I had a letter from my mother! She's coming to visit right after the Fourth! Isn't that great?" Ned says, turning his back to me as he digs in the junk drawer.

Wait. What? His mother is coming? I hope Piper picks up on my gesture of shooting myself in the head as a clear message that I detest this woman.

And there's "the one more" thing I don't need!

CHAPTER TEN

I f my mother-in-law wanted to be an actress, she could play any of the Disney villains without any direction. And she wouldn't be acting!

At first, she was warm and welcoming. After the rotten relationship I had with my mother, I thought I was finally going to experience good parenting. That all changed the first time I didn't want to celebrate a holiday the way she wanted; the gloves came off. Ah, that's where her son gets it ... reel 'em in and when it's too late, show your true colors.

She's also a snob who thinks the world revolves around New York and the East Coast. Everyone on the island knows she spent her youth here, and she is a Midwest person. She acts like she's "from" New York.

I don't think I've ever seen a quicker exit than Piper and Cam bolting out my door when she saw how I reacted to Ned's subtle proclamation. Piper was probably afraid I was going to explode at Ned right in front of her. Smart girl. And Ned's no dummy. He decided to tell me about his unwelcome news in front of them. How convenient he failed to mention it when we were alone. Play this cool, Nancy. Try having an actual conversation, like he's a reasonable adult.

"So, Mother Benson is coming for a visit? I'm a little surprised we didn't discuss it beforehand," I say. Keep your cool, Nancy. "Seems like you're pulling a lot of instant plans on me lately, and I'm the last to know."

"I'm sorry about that. I wasn't really asked as much as I was told," he says.

Could it be that Ned finally sees how pushy she is?

"I thought it was good timing because I did have to talk her out of coming in late September, which would have been right before your event," he says.

"That is something, I guess. A visit then would have been unbearable, and I would have insisted you tell her no."

"I mean, I only see her a few times a year, and she is my mother ..."

"Of course, you need to see her. Why doesn't she ever invite you to visit her in New York?"

"She does. All the time. She invites you too. You know New York is not my vibe. Rumor has it King Kong didn't fall off the Empire State building—he jumped. You are free to go visit her in the Big Apple anytime you want, but it's not for me."

Don't think humor is going to save you, Ned.

"Uh, that's a hard pass. I hope you realize I won't be much of a hostess with all my committee meetings coming up," I say.

I don't have any committee meetings that week planned, but I do now.

"Well, if you could join us for dinner most days, that would be appreciated," he says.

"I'll try."

"I mean, you can count on one hand the times you have to put up with her in the big picture," he says sheepishly.

Wait! Another glimmer he finds her difficult, too?

"Can I ask you a very direct question and get a very honest answer from you?" I ask.

Apparently, it's my day to be brutally honest with people.

"Don't you find your mother to be a bit boisterous and hard

to be around if you don't agree with everything she thinks or says?"

Wow. That's laying it out there.

"How would you feel if I asked you the same question about your mother if she were still alive?" he answers.

"Ask away. I wouldn't hesitate a moment. I'd tell you she was all of that and more. It doesn't change the fact she was my mother. Sometimes I can even be gracious enough to think she did the best she could, although that isn't saying much. She wasn't a good mother to me, and I would easily admit it," I say.

"Well, she's not here to say it in front of so it's a little different ..."

"I get it. She is your mother. I do the best I can, but I'm your wife. I don't think I should have to be pushed around because you won't be honest with her when she is out of line when it comes to me. For most of our marriage she hasn't been a cake-walk, I'll tell you that," I say, trying to keep my tone civil. "When it comes to taking a side between me and her, your actions always point to taking her side. How do you think that makes me feel?"

"I'm trying to keep the peace. I grew up with her. I know it is not good to go into combat with my mother. There's no winning. There's only wounds from the battle. Believe me, I have the scars to prove it," he says. "And so did my dad."

"You mean literally or physically?"

"I'm done talking about this. She's coming for a short visit and if we can get through it by smiling and nodding for the brief time she's here, it would be much appreciated. I have to get back to my project."

As the door closes behind him, I realize for the first time I don't know much about Ned's childhood. What happened to him?

CHAPTER ELEVEN

JULY 4TH

I know I have a red top somewhere in this closet, but I've spent so much time on the convention, I can't find it. The disheveled piles look more like a rat's nest, as my mother used to say when she described my housekeeping skills.

Funny how I thrive in chaos. Messy works for me. Drives Ned crazy. I bet every bolt and screw are alphabetized in his workshop. Thankfully, I find my top and I feel pretty festive in my red shirt, blue pants, and red, white, and blue flag necklace.

Besides, as Nancy showed all of us in *The Secret of Red Gate Farm*, sometimes you have to take a break from the arduous work for some fun. If she could play a game of croquet and horseshoes instead of sleuthing for a minute, I can take a break from convention planning. I want to have a good day. Walking to Piper and Cam's to start our afternoon festivities, I'm not even irritated by Ned's rare but nice compliment about my coordinated holiday outfit.

"You look pretty patriotic yourself in your red polo, blue jeans, and white deck shoes," I say, trying to be pleasant for the day ahead after his telling me I looked lovely.

As every young girl learned in *The Whispering Statue*, the male ego needs a compliment now and then. Ned's white deck shoes are a little "Pat Boone" for my taste, but I don't want to rain on his American parade.

"I know the white shoes are a bit much, but I was trying to get white in the picture, and this is the only way I could figure out to do it. Are you embarrassed to be seen with me?" he asks with a chuckle.

"As long as you don't start crooning 'Love Letters in the Sand,' we should be okay."

"You know that song? My dad played it all the time."

"So did my dad. It was his go to on the old hi-fi. He'd pour himself a cold one, put on some Pat Boone, and put up his feet. Then when my mother started to nag him about something that needed to be done in the house, he'd turn it up louder and pretend he didn't hear her. Made me giggle every time," I say.

Oh my gosh, I hadn't thought about Dad and the old hi-fi in years.

"Our dads could have hung out!" Ned says. "Well, here we are at Chez Nelson, Piper and Cam's home. Living next to the Grand is either really handy or maybe annoying with lots of tourists," he says.

"Probably a little of both. I've never been inside, have you?"

"No, I've talked to Cam out here on the sidewalk, but never inside either."

"Well, lookie here! Mrs. Nancy and Mr. Ned. Aren't you a handsome couple all in your red, white, and blue!" Freddy says as he opens the front door. "Come on in! Pip and Cam had to run to the shop for fifteen minutes because there was a small leak in a pipe that's been giving us trouble. They asked me to stay back. Come on in and have iced tea. They assured me you will still have plenty of time for your carriage tour. You're gonna love it. Our buddy Farnsworth is bringing his best carriage and horse so you can have a fantastic island ride on this glorious day!"

Stepping inside, it instantly feels cozy and comfortable with a slight bohemian feel. Pieces of Piper's artwork are displayed throughout the living room walls and the fireplace hearth has a row of Mackinac Island scenes painted in watercolor.

"Thanks, Freddy. Are you sure we aren't imposing?" Ned asks.

"Not at all. Have a seat. And let me grab the iced tea. I'll be right back," Freddy says.

"Look at all of Piper's work. These must be her favorites. Aren't they amazing?" I ask.

Quietly getting closer I whisper so Freddy won't hear, "Be ready. Freddy is going to tell you some jokes. He can't stop himself," I say, just before Freddy arrives with the iced tea.

"Here's the tea. Take a load off before Cam and Pip get back. Say, Ned, what's it called when you fry an egg with a bunch of other ingredients?"

"Well, I think that's called an ..." Ned starts to answer.

"Never mind, Ned. Omelet you figure it out," Freddy answers, barely able to get the words out before breaking into laughter. "Get it! *Omelet you figure it out!*"

"Wow, Freddy. You got me on that one," Ned says, glancing sideways at me.

My shrug should send the message; we're trapped.

"I did want to tell you; Cam broke his drum kit. I somehow managed to repair it, but now he has to deal with the repercussions!" Freddy says with comedic timing.

I'm waiting for the drum ricochet that usually follows a comedy act.

"Get it? Drum kit. Repercussion? Of course, Cam doesn't play drums, but I had to tell the story somehow."

"Freddy, do you secretly want to be a stand-up comic? Or maybe The Unknown Comic on *The Gong Show*? Remember that?" I ask, trying to get him to talk and not tell another groaner.

"Yes, I loved *The Gong Show*. Gene Gene the Dancing Machine made me laugh until I cried," Freddy says. "Knock, knock!"

Apparently, my conversation starter isn't working.

"Who's there?" Ned asks.

He doesn't seem that annoyed by Freddy. Maybe he was a *Gong Show* fan too. That's something else I have no idea about this man who is my husband.

"Cannoli."

"Cannoli who?"

"I cannoli imagine what you are going to do for the rest of the day!"

Now they are both laughing. And Ned is *really* laughing. Must be a guy thing.

"Did you know I started a business building yachts in my attic? Sails are going through the roof!" Freddy says.

Thank goodness. Piper and Cam have arrived.

"We are so sorry we couldn't greet you," Piper says bursting through the door.

"Yes, the plumbing at The Creative Lilac is going to be the death of me, but we got it fixed. At least for now," Cam says.

"Well, good, Freddy got you some iced tea," Piper says, sitting down next to me on the couch.

"Yes, Freddy has been the entertainment. Quite amazing," I say.

"Freddy! Have you been at the puns and knock-knock jokes again?" Piper asks.

"You know I can't stop myself, Pip. There's just too many good ones!" Freddy says.

"He gave me some good laughs, and I for one loved it," Ned says, patting Freddy on the back.

"Well, you folks have a dandy of a time. I'm gonna go over to the Jonas brothers' and chew the fat, and then watch the fireworks from the shore," Freddy says.

"Freddy, you know you're welcome to join us on the Grand lawn. We'd love to have you," Piper says.

She really seems to love the old guy.

"Oh, I know Pip. But I promised the guys, and besides,

you young'uns need some alone time with your friends. I'll see yah later, and it is so good to see you, Mrs. Nancy and Mr. Ned. You make a lovely red, white, and blue of a couple and I'm proud to know you, and proud to be an American," Freddy says stopping for a moment with a tear in his eye. "You know I love this country, and this island. I'm thankful, so thankful, to the good Lord for friends like you and this nation. God bless us and God bless the U.S.A.," he says with a salute.

Oh my gosh, the old guy has me choked up.

"But, let me leave you with this one story ..." Freddy says, speaking in a hushed tone. "There was a soldier who was shot during battle."

I wonder if Freddy served in the war. I never really asked him.

"Yes, he was shot in battle but some coins in his pocket stopped the bullet!" Freddy says.

"Oh, my goodness, was this someone you know?" I ask.

"Yup, those coins in his pocket stopped the bullet. It was his *life savings*." Freddy concludes.

Here we are, all leaning in to hear his heartfelt, patriotic story and zing! He hits us with another pun!

"Freddy, you rascal, time to leave. Get out of here," Piper says.

"Hee hee! Life savings!" Freddy can't stop chuckling.

"See you Fredster ... thanks for the laughter. You are one-of-a-kind!" Ned says.

All this laughter reminds me of Nancy's experience in *The Phantom of Pine Hill* and all the wisecracks her friend made to ease the tension of that case. Freddy the jokester can make the day light up.

"Have fun with the Jonas brothers," Piper says, closing the door as Freddy leaves. "Seriously, Cam, you have to talk to him. He hasn't listened to me."

"Piper, what can I say? He's discovered some newfound

enjoyment in jokes and puns, but I agree, he's out of control," Cam says.

"Oh, he's not so bad. I mean, the fact he can remember all of them at his age is pretty terrific," Ned says. "He was very entertaining. We mentioned to him that he should have been on *The Gong Show.*"

"Yes, well, he's the 'known' comic and he's driving people crazy!" Piper says. "I love him with all my heart, but let me explain to you what's happening here—what I've come to understand from reading about psychology. The technical term is—he's gone 'coo-coo for cocoa puffs!'"

"You are the person who has to hear it the most. I will, gently, try to talk to him," Cam says. "Maybe he'll get them all out of his system when he's visiting with his buddies today. We can only hope. But, hey, enough about Freddy. Are you two ready for a scenic carriage ride, or do you feel like you've seen all the nooks and crannies of the island already?"

"I've seen quite a bit, but I will have to say, I feel pretty negligent about not taking my wife to many of the lesser-known scenic areas. Is that a true statement, Nancy?" Ned asks.

I guess this tour will tell me how much I haven't seen. Sounds interesting.

"Thanks for inviting us, you guys. It was very nice of you," I say.

And, yes Ned, negligent is your modus operandi. But I have to admit, he is trying. It is working to not talk about the convention today. Everything I'm thinking of today somehow leads me back to another Nancy Drew book, and the lessons it teaches. In *The Haunted Showboat,* Nancy found out she could have great conversations that didn't necessarily include the current mystery she was working on. That's another Nancy life lesson that applies. Nancy Drew life lessons simply apply to everything! Wait, am I coming off like Freddy? Do I talk nonstop about Nancy Drew and drive everyone around me crazy? Am I "coo-coo for cocoa puffs," and no one will say it?

CHAPTER TWELVE

*T*hat was one of the best days I spent with Ned since we were married. It probably helped that we weren't alone, which doesn't seem to work for us. Piper and Cam are easy to be with. The carriage driver, Mr. Farnsworth, was so knowledgeable, along with Cam, and even Ned. All of them had little tidbits to throw in about the history of the island.

My favorite stop was at a place called Sugar Loaf. I enjoyed the clip clop of the horses as we headed to Sugar Loaf Road at Point Lookout. The pictures I've seen of this seventy-five-foot tall, towering rock formation didn't do it justice. It's supposed to be the tallest limestone stack on the island. According to Mr. Farnsworth, as the high waters of the lake drained away and eroded the surrounding rock, this is what was left. He said the Native Americans who see Mackinac Island as a sacred place have a different version of how it came to be that involves their culture and beliefs. He didn't know the whole story but told us to look it up at the local library where we could find out more. Funny, I've lived here for over two years, and I know very little about its history. Probably because no Nancy Drew books are set on the island.

Settling onto a blanket on the Grand Hotel lawn after such a magical carriage ride and watching the fireworks light up the sky over the sparkling water made my heart soar. When Ned took my hand, I didn't pull it away. I kind of wanted to, but at the same time, I didn't want to. I don't know what I feel. If he acted every day like he did while we were having such a fun day, I could see a future with him. But the Mr. Grouch I live with most days … I don't see walking into the sunset with that dude. I can't think about this right now. I have a week with my mother-in-law in the house and more to do for the convention. Still, it was a lovely Fourth of July.

Thankfully, the girls did agree to more meetings this week. Even if they didn't, I would have faked meetings to not be around while Mother Benson was here making poison apples, or whatever she does in her spare time. Which Nancy Drew villain would she be? Hmmmmm. I'll have to think about that one.

"So, you'll be here for dinner?" Ned asks. "Mother will be expecting that. Should we say 7 p.m.?"

Well, whatever Mother wants, Mother gets.

"I'll try to be back. When does she arrive?" I ask.

"She's planning on taking the 2 p.m. ferry over, so she will be here shortly. I'm picking her up at the dock."

Couldn't she just fly over on her broom? Oh, good thing I don't say everything out loud.

"I'll do my best," I say as I wave goodbye on my way out the door.

This time on my trek to The Creative Lilac for our meeting, I'm going to pay attention to the flowers along the way. They're all so beautiful, and winter will come back far too soon. I shouldn't be wasting one moment of their glorious blooms in their full July splendor. Even though the lilac trees seem mostly done for the season, there are several reblooming lilacs on my route that are "stop and sniff" worthy. That old book I found in the house on island flowers should help me identify some of these plants. I'm not going to let know-it-all Katherine be ahead of me on knowing about island flowers.

Yes, those are Marsh Marigolds. They look like bursts of sunshine. There's the Yellow Trout Lily. It seems some people use it as ground cover. Ah, the Meadow Cranesbill and Jacob's Ladder remind me of the water and the sky in their blue reflections. Oh, this island. Leaving Ned would most likely mean leaving this island. Hmmmm. I think I love the island much more than the man. What does that say?

Yikes! I'm going to be late with all this flower hunting. I have to get my brain back to business. Ah, there's the familiar tinkle of the bell at The Creative Lilac.

"Hi Freddy. Are all the ladies upstairs for our meeting?" I ask, approaching the checkout area. "What's this? A new sign?"

"Yes, I guess I've been going a bit overboard with my funny puns and jokes, so Cam suggested I place this sign," he says sheepishly.

Too funny. A sign that states: *Ask Me If You'd Like to Hear a Joke!*

"Well, have you had many takers?" I ask.

"Uh, a few. But it really has cut down on telling as many as I did. Maybe people needed a break, or so I've heard."

Ah, poor, sad Freddy. He seems a little forlorn.

"I want to hear a joke," I say.

I don't, but I can't take that sad face.

"You do?"

The torture is worth the happy look on his face.

"Hit me with your best one,"

"Well, it may not be my best one, but it's a goodie! Here goes ... I dropped ten dollars yesterday and chased it for miles. I never caught it, but at least it gave me a good run for my money," he says with such a look of expectation on his wrinkly face.

"Oh, that is a good one!" I say, mustering all the fake laughter I can.

"Get this one ... even if a bear wears socks and shoes, he still has bear feet!"

"Thanks for the giggle. I'll head upstairs now. You enjoy your day," I say.

Oh, Freddy, at least I hope I made your day better.

"I will!" he says, muttering, "bear feet, hee hee ..."

Sweet, sweet Freddy.

I hear the chatter as I get to the top step. These ladies are never at a loss for words. I like to arrive a few minutes late, so they have that chatter time, or we don't get down to business very fast. I know my girls!

"Hey ladies. So glad we are all together. How is everyone doing?" I ask, turning to face the gals.

"I'm having so much fun getting to know these ladies!"

What? Mother Benson is here with *my* girls? What in the world is she doing here?

CHAPTER THIRTEEN

"There's my daughter-in-law!" Mother Benson says, rushing at me with a hug.

"What are you doing here? Isn't Ned picking you up?" I ask, trying to sound cordial.

"Oh, I took an earlier boat, walked into town ... I called and left a message...and happened in here. I got talking to Freddy downstairs and told him who I was. He told me you were coming here for a meeting! It's kismet! I thought I would meet your pals. What great gals they all are!" she says.

Freddy, I listened to your stupid jokes, and you can't even give me a heads up? That's what I get for being nice. Oh great. Mother Benson has spent her time making herself look like the loving mother-in-law she isn't.

"Yes, well, do you want Ned to pick you up here? We have a meeting to attend to, and unfortunately, it's for committee members only. I'll look forward to catching up with you at dinner tonight ..."

"Yes, Mrs. Benson. It's been great having you here, but we have a lot to get to today, if you don't mind," Piper adds.

Thanks for reading the room and helping out, Piper.

"Oh, of course. You know me. I never want to be a bother.

Why don't I go downstairs and wait for Ned in the store. He should be here any minute," Mother Benson says.

The tone in her voice sounds cordial, but the look on her face is one I know well. Now, Miss Passive-Aggressive is irritated.

"We've been having a fun chat," Maxine says.

"Your mother-in-law sure has an interesting life in New York!" Marlene adds.

"Maybe she has some ideas for the convention we can incorporate," Gail says.

"Tell us more about all the committees you were on in New York, Mrs. Benson," Brenda says.

"Not a good time, ladies. Mrs. Benson is here to see her family, not work on a committee," Piper says.

Thank goodness for Piper. None of these ladies really understand what is happening here.

"Hey, Mother, good to see you! Sorry I didn't get here sooner!"

What a relief. There's Ned. At least he knew to get up here as fast as possible. He's afraid to look at me because he knows I want to kill someone right now, and he would be at the front of the line. Well, second. Right behind his mother.

"Let's let these ladies get back to their business, Mother. And I'm sure you want to get settled, so we'll be on our way," Ned says, trying to move her toward the stairs.

"I really thought perhaps I could be of help if I stayed for the meeting. Heaven knows I'm good at planning," she says with a stern look to Ned.

"Oh, come on, Mother, you're on vacation. Time to go!" Ned says with a panicked sound.

"Thanks for the offer, but enjoy the afternoon with your son," I say.

"Alright, then, if you insist," she says with that tone that always sits on my last nerve.

"Off we go then. Nice to see you all. See you at home, Nancy," Ned says.

The ladies murmur niceties and mother and son finally start down the stairs. As the ladies begin chatting once again, Piper gives me a knowing look of "oh, I'm so sorry that happened" and I give her a shrug back.

"This meeting is called to order. Let's go through some of the details from the agenda we set up," I say, ready to move forward from this disappointing day.

Oh, brother, more footsteps coming up the stairs. Can't the woman take a hint?

"Hello, ladies. How wonderful to have you all congregated here. It saves me from having to call each of you individually. I love it when things are easier, don't you?"

Are you kidding me? Now we are all in the gaze of the other lady who could have flown in on a broom. What do *you* want, Katherine Sims-Dubois?

CHAPTER FOURTEEN

"$\mathcal{J}$ thought I would be speaking only with Piper, but I ran into the Bensons downstairs who let me know you were having a committee meeting up here, so that works out splendidly for me," Katherine says as she swishes her skirt to the side to sit down without being asked.

Why didn't I hear the swishing as she was coming up the stairs? I'm too rattled, that's why!

"Katherine, are those horses on your skirt and horses on your shoes?" Gail asks.

"Why, yes, they are. I had a speech this morning at the Grand Hotel to the Equine Society of Michigan, and as you all probably have noticed, I dress for the occasion, always. It's *paaart* of my commitment to the island, and its people. I'm always the main representative for the islanders."

She can't say "part" like a normal person. There it is again. "Part" sounds like "pot" as she emphasizes the "t's" and those long vowel sounds. She'd make a great character in the comics. A laugh a minute, but I don't find it funny she showed up here unannounced. You really should try Earth sometime, lady. I think you might like it.

"Katherine, this is a private committee meeting. I'm sure there's nothing you have to say that couldn't wait …" I say.

"Don't be so sure. I thought you and your lovely committee would want to know that the Grand Hotel is on the verge of canceling your oh-so-cozy Nancy Drew convention! My sources tell me that your agreement was verbal only. Nothing was signed. And as luck would have it, someone else is interested in those dates and the Grand would stand to make a lot more money than they ever would with your little endeavor. Anyone with business sense would say 'tah-tah' to Nancy Drew and 'hello' to the almighty dollar. After all, it's not personal, it's business."

I would love to slap that smug look off her face and knock out a tooth or two.

"You do have a contract, don't you Nancy?" Marlene asks.

"The Grand would never do that to us, would they?" Maxine asks.

"Money makes the world go 'round, ladies. Always has, always will," Katherine says while admiring her brightly polished talons that pass for fingernails. "Well, I've done my duty by letting you know. Always glad to help. I so enjoyed seeing your faces when I passed on this news. Someday, certain people on this island will realize it's useless to try to keep anything from me, because I *always* win in the end."

Staring directly at Piper, everyone in this room knows exactly what she means.

No one says a word as we all watch the *swish, swish, swish* of the lady with ice in her veins exit down the stairs. Looking at the worry on all their faces, I need to reassure them fast.

"Ladies, you've just heard another one of Katherine's rumors. You should all know better than to believe anything Katherine Sims-Dubois hears through her contacts. She simply loves to cause trouble to anyone who doesn't bow to her every whim and wish, and as a group we don't … so there you go. Now, let's get to our committee meeting. Can we please?" I say.

It's a relatively quiet meeting where everyone sticks to the facts about their area. I imagine they are all wondering what is truly going on and who to believe. I need to get to the bottom of this, but I also need the loyalty of these gals. After the group disperses, it's just me and Piper, and I know she wants answers.

"What is Katherine up to, Nancy? I mean, that last comment was directed at me no doubt, but that should have nothing to do with you and the convention," Piper says.

"She's a troublemaker. She has no say over the convention. It's one more attempt to cause problems. We both know that's how she is," I say. "Piper, could I have some privacy to make some phone calls up here? I have phone cards, so it won't be charged to your phone, but with my mother-in-law at my house, well, you get it. Would that be alright?"

"Of course! Help yourself. I'm sorry about Freddy not alerting us to anything. The intercom is on the fritz. The plumbing, the intercom, Katherine … the enemy is working overtime lately," Piper says.

"When you say the enemy, you mean the devil…as in, the devil could be behind all these problems?"

Someone thinks it's Halloween!

"Remember when I said the devil prowls around like a roaring lion seeing who he can devour, and he dwells in discouragement? This fits the bill."

"It does all feel quite discouraging, I'll give you that," I say.

I'm trying to keep my spirits up and not look like I feel in front of Piper, but it's getting harder to not want to scream, kick something, or have a good cry.

"I'm going to be praying for you and the phone calls you need to make. I know this is stress you don't need, but God does walk through everything with us. That's how I survive the ups and downs of life," she says, softly touching my shoulder.

"Sure, pray, do a rain dance or whatever it takes. I'll take any help I can get. Between Katherine, my mother-in-law, my husband, and the pressure of getting this all underway, I feel alone."

"You are not alone. I am with you, God is with you, and the gals are all with you. Don't take their quietness for disloyalty. They just weren't sure what would be the best way to support you, I think. Feel free to make all the phone calls you need to, and don't worry about costs. No big deal. Come down when you're done. I'll make sure no one disturbs you," Piper says as she heads down the stairs.

Alone in the room, I can't help but shake. What is Penny doing? Didn't she make the down payment like she told me? Yes, I never officially turned in the contract, but surely that doesn't matter at this late date if they have the down payment. It all happened so fast once they had that cancellation. That was a bonehead move. Maybe *you* should try earth sometime, Nancy.

~

I don't know how to feel after talking to Penny. She said all the right words, but something is off. There was assurance after assurance that she had made the initial down payment, albeit a little later than I thought. Deciding to call my contact at the Grand right away was a good decision too. Yes, they had a follow up higher offer, but with my down payment having just arrived, they were sticking to our agreement. I could sense some tension about the money not coming when I thought, but at least we are still on track for our convention. Whew! Sounds like they *were* considering booting me. And, yes, we agreed I need to get the formal agreement turned in. Fine by me. I don't want to go through this again. That blasted Katherine! Jumping on any rumor she hears and upsetting everyone.

Penny mentioned running into my ex and that's when her voice got a little strange. I should have come out and asked her if she was interested in him. She should know better. I told her enough about the life I had with him. If she wants him, she's welcome to him. I can't take it. I'm calling her back and directly asking her.

"Hey, Penny, it's Nancy again," I say, trying to sound nonchalant.

"Hi Nancy, did we forget something? I promise, the next payments will all arrive in plenty of time and I'm sorry about the first delay. There were, well, circumstances that held things up," she says.

"That's what I wanted to ask about. You said you ran into my ex, and I have this feeling, or intuition, or something that you're not telling me everything."

Her silence speaks volumes.

"Yes, well, I guess there is a little more to it," Penny says.

"More to it as in you're dating him," I say.

Silence again.

"I was dating him. I'm sorry. I just didn't know how to tell you," Penny says.

"You said it in past tense ... it's already over?"

"Yes, and I should have talked to you before I got close to him. You know how handsome and charming he is. He showered me with tons of attention, was so interested in my life, and made me feel so special," she says softly.

"That gets all the girls at first. So, I take it he did something to make you break up."

"I don't want to get into details, but I caught him in a few lies. Then I started to think more with my head than my romantic heart and I did the smart thing. I told him we're through. I mean, we were only together a few months," she says.

"A few months? Why didn't you tell me?"

"Because I was having a fun time, and I didn't want you to spoil it. That's the truth. I should have talked to you, and maybe you could have talked some sense into me. In fact, that's why I was so late with the payment to the Grand. I was shirking my work duties, taking tons of vacation to hang out with him, and basically blowing off all the things I've worked so hard for. But that's all over now. I've seen him for what he is, and I've come to my senses."

"Well, be careful. He may not give up that easily. After all this time, he dropped some of our old love letters on me out of the blue, from our dating days. I still don't know what his point was," I say.

"He did mention he might do that. I could tell by his tone it wasn't out of love. I told him that wasn't nice, but I can see now he didn't listen to me. He seemed excited with the idea of getting you upset."

"That's what he's like. I'm sorry that he hurt you, but believe me, you're better off seeing him for who he is," I say.

"You'd think by this age I wouldn't be so gullible. He rushed into my life and swept me off my feet, but then couldn't keep up his act when I started to wonder about some things. I think he needs someone younger and with less life experience. I should have seen the red flags when he didn't mind me paying for everything. I was starting to catch him in lies," she says.

"Thank goodness he's out of my life and I'm glad he's out of yours. Don't let him back in. He will probably come back with some sob story, or elaborate reason you need to get back together. He did it to me time and time again. Don't fall for it."

"I won't, Nancy. And I'm sorry I didn't say anything, but it was over, so I thought maybe it would be best if I didn't bring it up. I did feel bad when you called about being late on the payment and not telling you what was going on. I'm hoping all is well with your convention plans?"

"Yes. I talked to the Grand after I talked to you. They did have another offer for a convention and if that payment hadn't arrived, I may have been axed. Thank goodness it all worked out. Trust me, you don't want to fall back with Mr. Wonderful, because he's a narcissist who only has his own interests in mind."

Saying goodbye to Penny, I do feel a little better but also quite irked that Phillip is messing up someone else's life. He probably has a woman in every port with a new scheme with each one.

"Everything okay?" Piper asks. "Sorry, I didn't mean to make you jump."

"Don't mind me, I was a million miles away. Thanks so much for letting me make my phone calls here. It sounds like there was some miscommunication about the first payment from my banking source, but it's all been cleared up now. Everything is good with the finances and the Grand. We are on track. I hate that Katherine found out anything about the convention, but it has worked out okay. I wonder who her mole is that heard what was going on and let her know right away," I say.

"I've often wondered that myself. She has a bunch of gals who keep their ears to the ground looking for any piece of news they think will tickle her ears. Most of the town is afraid of her and wants to stay in her good graces. She can be pretty cruel if she thinks you are crossing her. Just stay on your toes when it comes to her and the convention because she will try something. You're better off letting her think you're glad she is doing an opening speech. If you fight her, she will do something terrible," Piper says.

"Thank you for being here for me. Piper. It means a lot," I say.

"I'm going to keep those prayers coming. I think we're going to need them," she says.

"I mean, I'm not gonna lie. I'm starting to wonder if those prayers played a part in fixing this. I was about to have a panic attack. It looked pretty scary. Is that what it's like? You pray and presto, you get what you want?" I ask.

"I think you might be confusing Jesus with wishes from a genie in a bottle," she says with a wink.

"If God loves us, why not give us what we want … you know, like perks for people on His team?"

I know I'm sounding cheeky, but I do wonder.

"We are promised as believers that Jesus and the Holy Spirit are always with us, not the outcome we want in every situation. I would say on average, most things don't come out the way *I* think they should. That's where that faith comes into play again. It's not me telling God how my life should go. It's me asking God how I can join Him in His plans. That's a big difference. He walks through absolutely everything with us, but He said we would have troubles in this world. We aren't in Heaven yet. But make no mistake. When we are living for Him, all things ultimately work out for the good, even if they don't feel like it in the moment," Piper says.

"I guess if He did act like a big vending machine, He wouldn't know if people really cared about Him for who He is, or because of what He could do for them," I say.

"Exactly. I read this great book called *The Hiding Place* by Corrie ten Boom. It was the story of her life experiences in being actively resistant to the Nazis and her family's commitment to hide Jews in their homes during World War II. She and her family went on to experience the horrors of the concentration camp. They loved Jesus and I'm sure prayed they wouldn't have to take that path. But this is what I remember she said, along these lines: when a train goes through a tunnel and it gets dark, you don't throw away the ticket and jump off. You stay in your seat and trust the engineer. Jesus tells us through many stories in the Bible to not let this life's moments derail us, even when our expectations go unmet."

She hit the nail on the head when describing my life. Derailed!

Heading out to run errands before heading home, I have so many conversations swirling in my brain, I can't help but envision a big vending machine where you could pick your own mother-in-law. Now that would be a big selling point for the faith. Oh, my goodness. I really do need to read that Bible.

CHAPTER FIFTEEN

OCTOBER 2023

*L*ife has been a blur. There is no other way to describe the jump from summer to fall. I went from surviving my mothers-in-law's visit, where I concluded she could have easily been a villain in any Nancy Drew story to watching my gals give their all to bring the convention together. I've even taken a moment here and there to bask in the splendor of fall on the island. Ned has been decent, and things have really come together. Even Katherine has stayed out of my way.

I can't believe anywhere on Earth matches the vibrancy of the reds, yellows, and oranges that glow from the trees on the avenue leading up to the Grand. The brisk breezes as the temperatures drop with sweater-worthy days and crisp, chilly nights are a dream come true for anyone who loves autumn as much as I do.

Every time I drop tiny marshmallows into my cup of hot chocolate I think of Nancy's escapades in *The Mystery of the Moss-Covered Mansion* and all the many stories where she turned to the liquid heaven to relax after a day of difficult sleuthing. And like Nancy, I can't say no to a sumptuous piece of lemon meringue pie. Maxine offered to bring hot chocolate and her homemade lemon meringue pie to this meeting.

Like Nancy's friend Bess who worries about her weight, I think a diet may be in order after the convention. I've been digging into the treats nonstop lately. But no diet now. I need my stress eating to cope!

Making my way to The Creative Lilac, I want to savor these moments of happiness. Vibrant leaves, breezes across the Straits, the clip clop of the magnificent horses and the .... *swish, swish, swish.* No! I know what that means.

"I must say I am surprised. I thought for sure this would have fallen apart, but it looks like you're going to pull it off. Well, at least at this point, I hope so. We have no time for any embarrassment when it comes to protecting our precious island. You do have all your ducks in a row, don't you, Nancy, dear?" Katherine asks.

I'm not your dear, lady.

"Fancy bumping into you. Yes, I'm happy to say we are ready for a fabulous convention. In a few short days, many first-time visitors will experience the first Nancy Drew convention at the Grand Hotel. It will be a marvelous experience for everyone, I'm sure," I say.

"Well, my speech is prepared. First, I regale the book lovers with my own love of the Nancy Drew series. And then ..."

"You get two minutes, Katherine," I say cutting her off. "Two minutes and that's it. We are on a tight schedule, and they aren't coming to see you. Welcome them to the island and be done. I don't have to get one of those big hooks like in the old vaudeville days to pull you off the stage, do I?"

"As if! You're lucky I'm making time in my busy schedule to grace your audience with my wisdom!"

Yes, Katherine. You're a saint. Maybe on your car ride off the island you'll have to ride on the dashboard. Ugh, this lady!

"Feel free to skip it if you're too busy. Are those pumpkins on your skirt and shoes?"

"Yes. It's fall. It's pumpkin time. Of course, there are pump-kins on my skirt!"

"Don't tell me! There will be magnifying glasses on your skirt and shoes for the convention?"

"Well, if you must know, yes. That is the direction I'm thinking. Your guests should be thrilled that I not only take the time to grace them with my words, but also with my dedication to high fashion. Most people appreciate what I do, but I can see that you ... you ..."

"Ladies! So good to see you, Mrs. Nancy and um, Katherine."

With my gaze fixed on Katherine and thinking up one more snarky thing to add to our conversation, I completely missed Freddy coming up behind us.

"Say, Katherine." Freddy says. "Did I ever tell you about the time I slipped on a pumpkin? It caught me off gourd. Get it?? *Off gourd*. And, who helps the smaller pumpkins safely across the street? Why the *crossing gourd*, of course!"

"Freddy!" Katherine and I both say at the same time.

"Oh, sorry. It just came to me because of Katherine's skirt. I mean...pumpkins and all ... well ... gourdbye!" Freddy says making a quick exit.

Okay, that is funny. It seems my laughter is irritating Katherine. Good. She irritates me every time she speaks.

"That's my cue to exit, too. See you at the convention for your two minutes ... and .... gourdbye!" I say turning and walking as fast as I can the rest of the way to my meeting.

I think Freddy's crazy antics saved the day. I was about to smack Katherine. I've probably set myself up for some type of revenge, but boy, it felt good to give her some of her own medicine.

After a quick "hello" to The Creative Lilac staff person whose name I can't remember, I head up the stairs. Katherine has made me later than I wanted to be. It's calming to hear the laughter of my committee.

"Nancy! Wait until you see the height of the meringue on

the pie Maxine made for our meeting!" Brenda says as I'm reaching the top step.

"Once I started with the beaters, I couldn't stop. It was kind of cathartic." Maxine giggles, pointing to the tallest pie I've ever seen.

"Wait until you hear who I ran into on the way here …" I say.

Wait! Someone else is here besides our group.

"Nancy, sit down and I'll pour you a hot chocolate. Allow me to introduce you to Sister Mary Margaret," Piper says.

"Hello, Nancy. So nice to meet you. I've heard such good things about your skills and the upcoming convention. I'm so happy to be involved!" Sister Mary Margaret says.

This is not who I was expecting. The way Piper went on about her, I figured she was six feet tall. She's very tiny, the smallest woman in the room. And she's got red, curly hair pulled back into a small ponytail. At least she's not wearing a habit, but her modest, matronly dress and highly sensible shoes are also not the latest fashion. It must be the nun compromise for not wearing their usual garb.

"Nice to meet you, Sister Mary Margaret. I do still say Sister, right?" I ask. looking to Piper.

"Yes, we all call her Sister or Sister Mary Margaret. But the first time I met her, I called her 'Your Nunness'—remember that, Sister?" Piper asks as they both break into giggles.

"As Freddy says, as long as you don't call me late for dinner …" Sister says, still laughing.

"Speaking of Freddy, I have a story for all of you …" I say.

After telling the whole story, while making myself look charitable and Katherine like a monster—I can't help peeking around the room for reactions.

"My favorite part is the 'gourdbye.' That is too funny!" Brenda snickers. "Good 'ole Freddy. He really did save the day so you could make a fast exit from you-know-who."

"You know what this means, though," Marlene says.

"Yes," Gail adds. "She will be planning something. We all have to be on our toes and looking for it."

"You may need that vaudeville hook to get her to stop talking," Marlene adds.

"I guess I'd forgotten how interesting Katherine can be and her presence here. I've never had a true one-on-one conversation with her, but I think you handled yourself admirably, Nancy. You can't have her taking over your convention. You set some good boundaries, good for you," Sister says.

Yaaay me. I expected to get in trouble with "Your Nunness."

"Ahhh, she's a continual trial, isn't she? You did good, Nancy. Hopefully she will behave. With all of us watching out, it should be fine," Piper says. "For once, Freddy's jokes served a purpose."

"Actually, Piper, I was putting myself in a good light as I told the story. Truth be told, I was at my snarkiest because I just wasn't in the mood to humor her," I say sheepishly.

"Don't be so hard on yourself, Nancy. It's all going to be good. We are so close to the finish line. All this planning will pay off," Piper says gently.

"I almost forgot! I have a special surprise. As a thank you from the bottom of my heart, you are all invited to a dinner in the little private dining area right before you enter the main dining room. We'll be setting up all day, I know, but I want that time together to take a deep breath and enjoy being at the Grand. I want to get your dinner choices ahead of time so I can alert the chef, so I'll pass around a piece of paper for you to make your choices. I can't resist sharing these with you because they are so fantastic. Maxine, will you pass these out to everyone?" I ask.

As Maxine passes out the sheets, I can't stop myself from regaling all the choices for this sweet dinner.

"Okay, for appetizers, pick your choice from these four: seared boat scallops, butternut squash risotto, fresh chili, or ... pork and chestnut pate, farmers bread, and gooseberry mustard, or … frog legs Provencal, bean mélange, garlic aioli and anchovy crackle, or….pan roasted carrots, plant-based yogurt, and mint lemon pistachios," I say.

"It's so hard to decide. They all sound amazing!" Brenda says.

"And that's just the appetizers," I say. "Now, onto the soup and salad. Please write your choice of either grilled long stem artichoke and hearts of palm, or baby Caesar. For soups, choose between lobster bisque En Croute, duck consommé, or roasted fall squash."

"I'm going to faint from the grandeur of it all," Gail says. "Yum!"

"And now, dear ladies. The entrée choices. There's herb roasted leg of lamb, pan roasted chicken breast, slow roasted prime rib, pork osso buco, or cedar plank salmon."

"How will we be able to even work after this big of a meal?" Marlene asks.

"But wait! There's more!" I say, which gets a good laugh. "Don't forget about desserts!"

"Now you're talking," Sister Mary Margaret says with a giggle. I've only just met her, but I can sense what Piper says about her. She seems very special.

"Ladies, make your choice between vanilla bean crème brûlée, chocolate torte, Black Forest cake, cheese plate with fig preserves and baguette, or drum roll, please…"

They all take the cue and use their fingers to make a thunderous drum roll sound.

"The one and only, infamous Grand Pecan Ball!"

The drum roll now breaks into an even louder episode of laughter, whistles, cheers, and clapping.

"Thank you, ladies. Please fill out your sheets, and I'll take them with me and get them handed in. Really, from the bottom of my heart, thank you for helping and all you've done. Get a good night's sleep. In two days, please arrive at the Grand at eight a.m. with all your pieces of the puzzle, and we will begin the set up and finish all our preparations for the island's first and best Nancy Drew convention!"

I'm going to soak up the love, the cheers, and the joy in this room right now, because who really knows what the next few days will hold?

CHAPTER SIXTEEN

his is it. D-day for the first Nancy Drew convention in the history of Mackinac Island! Our October weekend is finally here! I'm impressed how these girls are full of energy to tackle the big set up that awaits us. The Grand staff is being so helpful to our crew. Cam, Ned, and Freddy have thrown in too, especially with the heavier lifting.

Registration is set up around the corner from the hotel check-in desk.

Done.

Registration packets and name tags are ready.

Done.

The Grand Ballroom looks exquisite with the large blow-up banners of Nancy Drew books near the walls, making for a festive feeling when entering the room. Everything we've added complements the large pink stripes on the walls. The round tables all have black tablecloths to add to the air of mystery, and Piper and her crew did an amazing job on each centerpiece. Each one is slightly different with a big magnifying glass as the main non-flower object. Cam helped with getting us a great deal on fall flowers. A single battery-operated candle in each center-piece adds to the ambiance and glow of perfect lighting.

"I have to say, if I was attending this convention, I would walk in here and be blown away," Marlene says, stopping for a moment to admire the room. "If you guys can spare me, I want to take one last look at the registration area before we eat. I want it to be perfect!"

"Go right ahead. I think we have this just about finished," I say.

"Yes! It's got the perfect combination of intrigue and fun, kind of like every Nancy Drew story!" Brenda says as she nods in agreement.

"This will go down as one of the best 'parties' we've ever put together for sure," Marlene adds.

"I'm exhausted, but so happy with how everything is turning out. All those meetings and planning are paying off. It's fun to see ideas become a reality, isn't it, ladies?" Gail asks.

"I couldn't be prouder of all of you," I say. "And, Piper, the art pieces and designs you've brought to the picture make everything shine. I can't thank all of you enough."

These ladies are the epitome of faithfulness and hard work.

"I feel the same, filled with thanks and gratitude to all of you. And, I have to say, that dinner we are having tonight is a mighty nice thank you. I can't wait!" Piper says.

"I know I haven't been here from the beginning, but I have to tell you, I have never seen any convention look and feel so magnificent as this one," Sister Mary Margaret says. "You have all done this convention, and this island, proud by giving your gifts to the event. It's breathtaking!"

"And our rooms! They are magnificent!" Brenda says. "Tell them about our room, Gail."

"It's the most beautiful baby blue carpeting with accents of gold and white throughout the room. I would never put these colors and patterns all together, but they work here. I'm taking so many pictures. I never want to forget this room," Gail says.

"Marlene and I love our room too. The walls are an azalea color with marigold trim everywhere. It reminds me of the marigolds on the island. There are pictures and touches of geraniums, too. You're right, Gail. I've never seen anything like these rooms. I keep peeking inside the slightly open doors being cleaned as I walk down the hallway. I've seen lighthouses, dragons, floral patterns ... and oh, the canopy beds. How will we ever leave?" Maxine says.

"Nancy!" Marlene says, rushing back toward me. "We have some early registrants who want to speak to you. They didn't pre-register but told me they have exciting news to share with you. Can you come and see them?"

I knew there would be some last-minute guests, but these people are early. Hopefully, we can work it out.

"I'm right behind you. This is a good example of how we might have to adapt to last- minute changes," I say, walking behind Marlene. "We have to stay sharp, and we will figure it all out."

"Uh, this is quite a crew. I think you'll be surprised," she says.

She's right. I'm not quite prepared for the small crowd waiting at the desk.

"*Bon soiree*. You must be Nancy. Your assistant Marlene was good enough to fetch you for us."

"Hello, yes, my *team member* Marlene said you are here for the convention, but registration begins tomorrow. And I'm not sure there are enough rooms here at the Grand to accommodate this many people. Stop in tomorrow when registration opens and we can iron out the details for a stay, and of course you are welcome to attend the convention," I say, feeling confused.

"Oh, dahling, we already have our rooms secured. We are Mr. and Mrs. Mason. I'm Dolly Mason and this is my husband, Perry."

Perry Mason? Really? You've got to be kidding me.

She's a foot taller than he is and seems to love frocks with sequins like Dolly Parton. He's doing a good imitation of a short and pudgy Sean Connery, right down to the accent. Grabbing my hand and kissing it with an *"enchante,"* they sure do make quite a pair. And how many people are with them? Three more?

"These are our assistants, Carrie, Larry, and Sherrie," Perry says.

Am I in a keystone cop movie? Three stooges? What is happening?

"Everything okay?" Piper asks, joining the scene. "Need anything from me?"

Her expression tells me she is sensing something strange, too.

"This is Mr. and Mrs. Mason ... Perry and Dolly Mason and their assistants Carrie, Larry, and Sherrie," I say with a side look I hope she gets.

"Yes, we are here for the convention, and we are here to offer something magnificent for this crowd to see! Being quite the collectors, I have here, before your very eyes, a first-edition *Mystery at Lilac Inn* signed by none other than Carolyn Keene herself!" Dolly says, pulling the book out of her oversized, sequined bag.

"Speechless, right? We thought you might be!" Perry says.

"We didn't put much time into getting things like first editions. There were so many other details to take care of," I say. "We all love Nancy Drew, but mostly reading the books, especially as we were growing up. We aren't experts on all the publishing and that sort of thing. That's why we are having speakers who are experts. This is our first convention, so we are thrilled you brought us this treasure. Good thing you knew how to find it."

I'm stammering and yes, I am speechless.

"Oh, you have to know the right people, and *be* the right people to have access to things like first editions," Dolly says.

"And that's not all, Nancy. We are here to tell you that *we* are your angel investors! Yes, we are here to see the very convention we helped fund," Perry says.

"Um, let's not continue this conversation here. Mr. and Mrs.

Mason, would you follow me to a private room over here? I think that's where we should talk," I say, gesturing to a small room near the registration area. Piper and Marlene will work with Sherrie, Carrie...and well...all the rest of you to get you your registration packets."

Guiding the pair away to the room I can see the look on Marlene and Piper's faces as they hear the words "angel investors." I'm also mortified to see Cam and Ned rounding the corner and going past the registration area. Oh, please Piper and Marlene...don't tell them anything about angel investors. Please, please don't utter a word!

CHAPTER SEVENTEEN

"*D*ahling, you look flushed. Aren't you happy to see us? We thought you would love this surprise!" Dolly says.

"Yes! Meeting your angel investors and the chance for your convention attendees to see a first edition. Thrilling, right?" Perry adds.

"Of course, I'm happy you could make it. I'm just curious why you didn't contact me; I could have set up accommodations. We could have planned to let people know you were bringing the book," I say, hoping I'm covering up my shock.

"We love the element of surprise! And we have so many investments, we don't pay attention to half of them. We do live the life of the rich and famous. I know it sounds a bit snooty I know, but that's the case," Dolly says. "We've always thought about visiting the island and surrounding area, so this was perfect. You see, that's why we didn't need to have *you* make any arrangements at the Grand. We have assistants for that type of thing."

"The book is truly amazing, especially since we don't have any other first editions on display. Did you realize that Maxwell D. Powers will be coming in tomorrow?" I ask.

"Yes, Maxwell D. Powers. He's the one who is known for ..." Dolly says tentatively.

"All things Nancy Drew," I say, finishing the part that seems to elude her.

"Yes, that's him. It's been quite a trip and I know so many influential people. My brain froze for a moment," Dolly says.

"I bet he would love to take a look at this first edition. If anyone can give you more information about it, I'm sure he can," I say.

I hope they didn't see my ignorance when it comes to first editions. I need them to think I'm doing a great job.

"Well, how about that, Dolly? *The* Maxwell D. Powers will be here tomorrow, and ready to look at our treasure!" Perry says. "You know him. We've followed his career for years!"

"Of course! You know how I get flustered when I travel, Perry," Dolly says.

"Listen, guys, the angel investor thing is something only I know about. So, as happy as I am to have you here, please don't mention that to anyone else. I've kept the convention financials private, and I'd like to keep it that way for my own personal reasons," I say.

"Oh? Secretive, huh? No problem. We'd be happy to keep your secret," Perry says with a smirk.

Everything about these two is unnerving, and they certainly don't seem like who I thought the angel investors would be. But who am I to question them? Their eccentricity is why I was able to pull this off, so I better become grateful really quick.

"I appreciate your discretion. Let's keep the first edition quiet too. That way I can announce it as a major surprise after Maxwell does the keynote speech tomorrow evening. That will give my committee time to set up a proper place to safely display the book with lighting. How does that sound?" I ask.

"Perfect. Yes, after Mr. Powers' speech will be perfect. It will be exciting for the crowd," Dolly says. "Here it is for your safe-keeping."

"Thank you. Now what can I do to make your stay more comfortable?" I ask.

"I'm sure you have a million things to attend to. We actually got here early because we have other things we'd like to do off the island, back on the mainland. You won't see much of us until the main event tomorrow night. We'll stay out of your hair and let you attend to your convention details. I'm assuming you are going to meet all your financial goals?" Perry asks.

"Yes! We have a full slate of attendees, and all the financial obligations will be met. Thanks so much for investing. It couldn't have happened without you. I'm very grateful," I say.

They don't need to know I'm afraid we will be a bit short.

"Our pleasure, dahling. Now we must gather our crew and get settled in. With all our other plans off the island, we won't be in your way," Dolly says as we all stand up to head back to the registration area.

Whew! Cam and Ned are no longer lurking around.

"Come along, troops. Time to get settled in," Perry says to his entourage.

Like obedient little soldiers, they all stand up straight and move away from the area.

"*Au revoir*, dahling!" Dolly says as she sheds sequins with every step of her exit.

I remember losing sequins at dance class. I always thought it was because my mom got my costumes at the thrift store. I guess even rich people sequins don't stay put.

"Where did Marlene go?" I ask Piper.

"She went to see if the others needed help to finish up before dinner. Are you okay, Nancy? And what was that about? Angel investors? That group? Wow. Not my idea of what angel investors are like."

"Uh … yeah. I guess they just march to the beat of a different drummer. Piper, you didn't say anything to Cam and Ned about hearing about the angel investors here, did you?"

"No. I'm still sticking to everything you said about the

finances being private, and Marlene and I both agreed we don't need to say anything to the other girls. I'll keep my eye on these new guests and make sure they are happy," Piper says.

"That would be much appreciated. Thankfully, it sounds like they won't be back here until the main event tomorrow. They said they have their own rooms and reservations and lots of plans off the Grand grounds. We shouldn't have to worry about them. Isn't that something about them bringing the first edition?"

"Super exciting!" Piper says, clapping.

"Do you think you'd have time to put it in one of those plexiglass boxes we have and make sure it's well lit? I think that would add to the excitement. I told them we won't be revealing it until after Maxwell's talk tomorrow night. Oh, and if the other girls ask, just tell them it's another surprise and they'll find out soon enough. Does that work for you?"

"Absolutely. No problem. I am so used to doing displays in the store, I know exactly what to do. Wow. Dolly, Perry, Sherrie, Carrie, and Larry. Kind of like a traveling circus, but I don't want to look a gift horse in the mouth. There's a little sequin trail, did you notice?" Piper says, giggling.

"I did. She needs to go to some higher end designers," I say.

"Still, the fact they came is incredible. You must be pretty happy they are taking such an interest," Piper says.

"Yes, it's wonderful," I say. "My financial liaison said angel investors tend to stay behind the scenes, so I had no idea. Since they are Nancy Drew enthusiasts, I can imagine they were excited about bringing that first edition to the convention. At least they sound like they won't be in the way, even if they will attract attention by their very appearance."

"Really rich people are often also really quirky from my experience," Piper says.

"Look at what time it is! It's time to eat that sumptuous meal we have all been dreaming about. Would you mind rounding up the team and heading for our dining area? I'll be right behind you," I say.

"No problem. I'll see you there," Piper says.

Watching Piper leave to gather the girls, I can only hope these investors remain satisfied and don't cause any issues this weekend. Now I have more to do this weekend—namely keeping that entourage away from Ned. His offering to help suddenly doesn't seem so helpful.

CHAPTER EIGHTEEN

I must be dreaming. The dinner last night was delightful. The registration today has been going like clockwork. Ned and Cam have stayed out of the way, as have the angel investor crew. The Grand Ballroom is perfect, and the displays are garnering adoration from the attendees. Even the phone call with news that Maxwell would be a little late because of car trouble hasn't rattled me. Thankfully, I padded his arrival time just in case something came up. He won't have as much relaxation time before his speech, but it should still be on time.

Piper said she's been praying, and I believe it! It's good to have all those praying girls on my side.

"Nancy, I'm pleased to tell you Maxwell Powers has finally arrived. I just got the notice on the walkie-talkie that he's on the grounds from my lookout at the check-in desk. I know you were worried!" Gail says. "I'll go get him now and you can touch base. I'll meet you in the Grand Ballroom."

"Perfect! Whew, that is a relief. Can you imagine having our main speaker not show up? But he's here now and that's all that matters," I say.

Seeing him come through the door, he's exactly as I pictured him. A man of small stature, a coat with patches on the elbows, round spectacles with thick lenses, and a bow tie. Graying at the temples adds to his distinguished "professorish" look.

"Mr. Powers, what a pleasure to meet you in person," I say, extending my hand. "I'm Nancy Benson, and we are all so pleased you are here safe and sound."

"Hello, Mrs. Benson."

"Nancy, please."

"And please, call me Maxwell."

"I'll leave you two to your business. Lovely to meet you, Maxwell," Gail says.

"Thank you, Gail." Maxwell says.

"How was your trip over?" I ask.

"Oh, pretty good. I'm sorry for my late arrival. I had some car trouble on the mainland, but thankfully, I was able to get here in time. Anything I should know before my talk? I think what I have to say is going to be quite a revelation to the crowd. I'm going to be revealing what I know about the true authors of the Nancy Drew books, with the latest news that some people may never have heard," he says.

I can't concentrate on what he's saying, so I'll just keep nodding and smiling. Oh boy, there's some of the investors milling around. Thank goodness Maxine seems to be keeping them occupied. If I stash Maxwell in the greenroom off the stage, that should work. Giving the gals all instructions about who should be allowed to talk to who last night, even though they looked confused, was a good call. Very "Nancy" of me to cover all my bases!

"Sure, whatever you have to say is great. How are you feeling? Ready to tackle this group of Nancy Drew lovers?" I ask. "Follow me. I have a private room where you can collect your thoughts."

"I feel great! I'm filled to the brim with enthusiasm for this opportunity," he says beaming.

"Confidentially, I have a delightful surprise for you and the rest of the crowd once your speech is over. We were able to secure a rare, first edition of *The Mystery at Lilac Inn*, signed by Carolyn Keene herself, no less!" I say, lowering my voice so others near us won't hear.

"Surprising! I think after you hear my talk, you will understand why that's even more incredulous. May I see the book now?"

"I'm sorry, but I'd prefer to wait until after your speech. It's safely stashed under a plexiglass case for my announcement to the crowd. You'll have time later to see it," I say firmly.

The last thing I need is him getting distracted before his talk.

"Professor Powers, is it?" I hear the voice of Dolly Mason behind me at the same time I see Maxwell's eyes getting larger.

Darn it! I thought I could get him to the greenroom before they saw him.

"Oh, Dolly and Perry! May I present Maxwell Powers, our main speaker this evening," I say.

"Yes, we were thinking we might meet the professor in that guest room off the main stage that we scouted out when we were wandering around, but your lady seems to want to rush us off to some other area which we were not quite happy about!" Perry says, looking sideways at Maxine who shrugs and has a sorry look my way that seems to simply say: "I tried."

"It's not Professor, just Maxwell. Nice to meet you. You're both Nancy Drew fans I take it?" Maxwell asks.

I'm not a mind reader, but he too has the look of wondering where these two came from with their sequins and gaudy attire.

"We were, in fact, the ones who brought the rare, first edition Nancy Drew book to the convention. We're sure you will be thrilled to see it!" Dolly says.

"I would like to see it because you see, that's a very curious statement ..." As Maxwell looks like he's going to go into something lengthy, I have to cut him off.

"There will be plenty of time the rest of the weekend, but right now, we need to get you to the greenroom so you can freshen up, get a refreshment if you wish, and be ready to take the stage in a matter of minutes," I say, taking his arm and heading toward the greenroom and turning back momentarily to bark an order. "Maxine! Take the Masons to their seats of honor so they can get settled."

"For sure, please follow me," Maxine says with a furrowed brow, most likely because of the tone I don't usually use around these ladies. "We have the best seats reserved for you and your group. Uh, where are the rest of your group?"

"Oh, they'll be here any moment. Fine. Show us our seats, but we can't wait to talk with you, Maxwell," Dolly says.

"Yes. We can't wait!" Perry adds.

Even though it's like herding cats, I'm happy to see they do follow Maxine.

That was close! Now, if Maxine can make sure the other three stooges stay in the main ballroom, things should work out just right. Oh no! Ned's here!

CHAPTER NINETEEN

*I*f it's possible to politely shove someone in a room, I just did it.

"Here we are, the greenroom. Rest up, Maxwell," I say. "Carrie, Larry, and Sherrie, what are you doing here?"

"We were thirsty. After all, aren't we VIPs?" Larry asks.

"Nice spread," Sherrie says.

"Delicious," says Carrie with a mouthful of food.

"Don't worry. We only drank the punch. We didn't touch the iced tea clearly marked for your guest of honor," Larry says with a frosty tone. "Although, I also love iced tea. Would have been nice to have some for the rest of us."

"This room is meant for Maxwell. And you aren't supposed to be here," I say with an edge in my voice.

Maxine must have set that up for him. I remember asking her to find out any preferences Maxwell might have.

"Thank you. I do love my iced tea, and I am parched," Maxwell says.

"Well, these people were just leaving. You three can meet him later," I say. "Dolly and Perry are looking for you guys."

"They are?" Carrie asks, grabbing another handful of crackers as she quickly heads toward the door.

Larry and Sherrie follow behind, each grabbing a handful of snack mix as they finally leave.

"Whew. Sorry about that," I say. "Now you can have a few moments to collect yourself, enjoy your tea, and rest. I'll be introducing you shortly."

"Thank you, Nancy. I appreciate it. That's quite a bunch!"

"Yes, well as we learned in *The Clue in the Old Stagecoach*, tea can be very soothing after a rough experience. And those three are definitely rough around the edges," I say, hoping to lighten things up before he speaks. "Best you stay in here now, and I will knock on the door when it's time for you to walk on stage. How does that sound?"

"Perfect. I'll enjoy this tea and gather my thoughts. Thanks!" Maxwell says.

Okay. Back to the ballroom. On to the next potential disaster—keeping Ned away from the investors. If they find out he's my husband, they'll tell him who they are, and I can't have that.

"Ned! Ned!" I say, grabbing his arm and turning him toward the back of the room, away from where they are seated.

"Hey, I'm glad I found you. I've been trying to get a minute of your time, Mrs. Busy-Busy. By the way, who are those people in the front? I've not seen them around the island, and they sure are an interesting crew. Is that lady trying to look like Dolly Parton?" Ned asks.

"Just fervent fans marching to the tune of their own drum, I guess. They are very talkative, and I know you hate chit-chat, so you'd better not start a conversation with them, or you'll be there for hours! Now, why did you need me?"

I hope he doesn't notice I'm talking as fast as a chipmunk and my voice is rising, too.

"You know how I love everything aurora borealis?" Ned asks.

"Yes ... northern lights for us English-speaking people ..."

"Nancy, really?"

"Sorry, go on."

Get to the point Ned! I have a conference to run!

"Tonight is supposed to be spectacular, and the view from the porch should be ..."

"Nancy, sorry to interrupt, but Swishy-Swishy is in the building, and you said you wanted to know," Brenda says looking flushed. "Sorry, Ned, didn't mean to cut you off."

"Oh brother, I better attend to her. Ned, what about the northern lights?" I ask while starting to walk away.

"This crowd should see it. This can be a once-in-a-lifetime event for most people. They really should see it," he says.

"Yes, sure, they should see it. I'm sure they'll all see it later ..."

"So, I should let them know, don't you think?" Ned asks.

"Yes, whatever you think. But right now, I have to get to Katherine Sims-Dubois," I say rushing to meet her before she spots the investors.

"Katherine! Right on time. I'm just about ready to begin, so I'll introduce you momentarily," I say. "Lovely skirt. Those magnifying glass images on the hem and on the tips of your shoes are right on target. Now, you don't see that every day."

"Of course, you don't! I wish the rest of the world would sharpen up their image a bit," she says with a distinct air of disdain I can only imagine is aimed at my simple white blouse, black slacks, and blue blazer.

"Remember, two minutes. No longer. I've got my old vaudeville show hook primed and ready if I need it," I say with the sincerest chuckle I can muster while motioning a big yank.

"Hmmmph. That would be the day. Speaking of drawing attention ... what's up with the people in the front? Circus people?" Katherine asks, careening her neck toward the spectacle that is the Masons.

Oh, my word. Circus people. She's the clown.

"Just enthusiasts. You of all people should know some people like to dress, well, lively. But you're right. Nowhere near your place in society. I'm sure you don't hang out much with those types of ragamuffins," I say. "They are very crude and so beneath you. Best you steer clear."

I have to keep her from questioning them and finding out who they are.

"Time to head to the stage, Katherine. And remember. These people are here for the Nancy Drew convention. As much as we all love the island, it's not time for a lecture," I say with a stern look.

"Yes, so you say. Well, then. Time for me to have the microphone, isn't it?" she says in her fakey, saccharine voice.

This is it. This is how I felt that one time I was on a high ledge. Everything in my body is sweating. Following her to the stage, I do admit, if there was a ledge nearby, I would be tempted ...

CHAPTER TWENTY

"$\mathcal{A}$s the town chairwoman, it is my honor to welcome each of you to our magical island, where I'm happy to say we have very few real-life mysteries to solve. We love having all of you."

With a quick stop to knock on the greenroom door, I'm happy to hear her doing what I asked.

"It's time, Maxwell!" I say.

"Yes, good. Wow. Do I ever have a stomachache all of a sudden," he says opening the door and following me towards the stage clutching his iced tea glass along with his folder.

"Oh, I'm sure it's jitters," I say.

"Yes, probably. I feel weak too."

"Take another big drink of your tea. That will help."

"Okay, thank you."

Watching him take big gulps, I hope this is part of his usual process before speaking.

"Here we go," I say as we reach the stage.

Thankfully, Katherine stuck to two minutes. She said pleasant things about the island and the attendees, and I'm shocked she actually did her job efficiently. I even noticed a little less of pushing the Transatlantic schtick in her pronunciations.

Taking my place at the podium, I'm full of butterflies as I list off Maxwell's credentials. I may be crazy, but I think you can feel the electricity in the room as we are about to begin.

"Ladies and gentlemen and Nancy Drew lovers from all over, please welcome our distinguished expert speaker this evening, Maxwell D. Powers."

As he approaches the podium, he's pale, sweating, bending over slightly, and clutching his stomach.

"Thank you for inviting me to this Nancy Drew convention on this beautiful island," Maxwell says. "I hope you find what I have to share to be interesting and informative. Thank you to Nancy Benson and her committee. It's a pleasure to be here."

He seems to be clearing his throat and talking in a much more stilted style than when we chatted before. I must admit, he looks like he's in pain.

"Excuse my voice. I don't usually have such a frog in my throat. *Cough, cough.* It's no wonder so many people have such a fondness for Nancy Drew. She taught us about solving problems, and that we could choose to be anything, including an adventurous detective."

This brings applause from the crowd. Good point, Maxwell! This is the kind of stuff we like to hear.

"No doubt, many of you still think of Carolyn Keene as the author of the Nancy Drew series, and indeed she is, in a way. You may or may not understand it's only been in the past few years that it was revealed to the world that Carolyn Keene is in fact a pseudonym!" he says. *Cough, cough.*

There's a small but audible gasp in the room. Even though the news had come out during a court case a few years ago, it wasn't like Tom Brokaw had it as a headline story on the evening news. I read something about it in a small article in *The New York Times* carried by the library—not a common subscription for most people in our region. Nancy Drew lovers like me and my girls didn't even talk about it. We preferred to keep the books encased in our childhood memories with no changes.

Revealing anyone other than Carolyn Keene to be the author feels like saying Santa Claus isn't real! In my mind, Carolyn Keene will always be the pen behind the magnificent stories.

Cough, cough. "Perhaps you didn't see the obituary that appeared in *The New York Times* in March of 1982—a mere year ago—that Harriet Stratemeyer Adams passed away at eighty-nine years old. But go back further, and you'll learn about Edward Stratemeyer, the father of Harriet and her sister."

Now Maxwell is sweating so hard he has to mop it off. He's using the paisley pocket square from his jacket. Yikes! I know this is the guy everyone was talking about in a few of the Nancy Drew newsletters I skimmed, but I think I should have done a little more investigating on what he would talk about. He's going down a rabbit hole not all of us enjoy. And why is he coughing so much? It's distracting.

"Edward is the man who created Nancy Drew. He used his daughters Edna and Harriet as ghostwriters initially, but there was another. Her name is Mildred Wirt Benson. Remember that name. *Cough, cough.* Mildred Wirt Benson, I would argue, is the *real* creator of our famous sleuth. At the very least, she contributed greatly to twenty-three of the first thirty Nancy Drew mysteries. She's the writer who brought us a more adventurous, determined, and fierce Nancy than was originally conceived by Edward Stratemeyer. *Cough, cough.* Excuse me, oh my stomach …. "

Weird. Someone with the last name of Benson has something to do with writing Nancy Drew books!

"He seems to be ill, doesn't he? He wasn't like that a short while ago," Piper whispers to me and Sister. "Wait, he said Benson. Is she related to Ned and you?"

"No, it's a common name, like Smith. We aren't related. But look at Maxwell. He's flushed and sweating up a storm. He seems to be getting sicker by the minute, like he's catching some kind of instant cold or flu," I say. "I don't know how long he can go on like this."

"I'm so sorry," Maxwell continued. "I very rarely get sick, and this seems to be taking me over. Now, where was I? Yes, through my own extensive research, and some information from my aunt who is a librarian in Iowa, I believe this needs to become common knowledge to anyone who reads Nancy Drew books. In fact, I found that ... *cough, cough* ... "

"He's passing out!" someone from the crowd yells.

"Call the island ambulance, Piper!" I shout, running towards Maxwell.

He faints before I can reach him, hitting the podium on his way down. Blood is flowing from his head.

"I can help until paramedics get here," Sister Mary Margaret says, tearing off her vest and wrapping it around Maxwell's head. "I've done triage plenty of times in the field."

Thank goodness because I don't know what to do except try to keep this crowd calm.

Grabbing the mic, I hope my voice sounds steady and in control.

"Please, everyone remain in your seats. An ambulance was called. If there's a doctor in the house, we welcome your help. Everyone else remain seated so the paramedics can get to the front easily. I'll give you further instructions once we have him taken care of."

There doesn't seem to be a doctor in the crowd. What is going on? The man was fine fifteen minutes ago. What could have brought all of this on? No one else seems to be sick. Did he have some bad fish before he came?

Oh, good. The paramedics. It's unsettling to hear they are going to stabilize him and use a chopper to get him to Traverse City as soon as possible. As they wheel him out, I need to do something to get this back on track. There's a hushed buzz among the crowd and everyone looks frightened.

"Ladies and gentlemen, I'm so sorry this happened to Mr. Powers, and our prayers are with him. He's in good hands and on his way to the best medical care," I say.

As Piper gives me a knowing nod toward the back of the room where the display is set up for the rare book, I see she has turned on the spotlight over the area covered up with a black cloth. I think I know what she's thinking. I agree with her nod that this is the time to "change the subject" for these rattled attendees.

"While we continue to keep Mr. Powers in our good thoughts, please turn your attention to the back of the room. Did you notice the black draped cloth over the display with the bright light shining on it? We have a surprise for you! We have been blessed with a rare first edition copy of *The Mystery at Lilac Inn* for you to observe! Kindly turn your attention to the unveiling of this treasure!" I say.

The light overhead of the display gets even brighter, and Brenda pulls off the cloth to reveal the book in all its glory. A unanimous roar comes from the crowd who are excited to see the book up close. As expected, people scurry toward the back of the room.

"Take a good look, because we're going to open up the display, with white gloves of course, and show you the front, back, and inside," I say, happy this distraction is working.

Wait, why is Ned coming to the podium?

"I got this, Nancy!" he says as he whispers to me. "They don't want to miss this!"

Grabbing the microphone, he clears his throat. Ned, what are you doing?

"Ladies and gentlemen, before you get engrossed in the book, I implore you to head out on the porch for a very small window of beauty from nature that has presented itself! The aurora borealis —the northern lights as they are called—are putting on a spectacular show right now fully visible from the Grand Hotel porch. You don't want to miss this! I highly recommend you calmly head for the porch right now and take a look for yourself. The colors will blow you away," Ned says as he leaves the stage and begins to head for the door.

"Ned! What are you doing? We're in the middle of a convention here right after a traumatic moment ..." I ask, trying to keep up with him while also trying not to look panicked.

"Nancy. Don't miss this. Everyone else is interested. Can't you leave Nancy Drew behind for one minute to live in the moment and be Nancy Benson?" he says, outpacing me and heading for the porch.

Watching the room totally drain of people, including my team, I guess there's nothing to do but go see this "big deal" for myself. I'll follow the lesson of Nancy Drew in *The Secret of the Old Attic*; every once in a while, let your guy take charge.

CHAPTER TWENTY-ONE

*N*ed is right. There are no words for this. Spread across the Grand porch, there are only reverent whispers about what is before our eyes as we gaze toward the Mackinac Bridge. The sky is full of swirls of greenish-blue lights with touches of purple that ebb and flow like a perfectly choreographed dance. Waves of light shimmer like curtains and clouds across the horizon, brightening and fading but continually taking my breath away.

"How can you see this and not believe in a loving God?" I hear Piper whisper to Cam.

"Did you know it could be this very type of thing that Ezekiel saw and mentions in the Bible as a 'whirlwind coming from the north with brilliant light and gleaming,' and he also mentions fire flashing," Sister Mary Margaret says joining in their conversation.

"The auroras are an interaction of the solar wind and the Earth's magnetic field," Ned says to me, loud enough so others can hear.

Thanks, Ned. You dampened the magic. I think I like Cam and Piper's idea better. This is in the Bible? I wonder.

After a good amount of time to take in the show, I think it's time to move on.

"Piper, will you help me get the people back inside? I feel like we need to get this all back on track," I say moving closer to Piper and the team who are huddling around her. "If all of you will help, that will be best, I think."

"Ladies and gentlemen. This certainly has been an amazing treat, and hopefully it will be sticking around for a little while, but I do believe we need to get on with the rest of our evening's program. I'm so happy you were here to see the northern lights. If you would all make your way back to the Grand Ballroom now, we'll resume in about ten minutes," I say, gesturing for the crowd to move back to the Grand entrance.

"Okay ladies, let's get this show back on the road ... Piper, Maxine, Marlene, Gail, Sister...we can do this. Hey, where's Brenda?" I ask as we try to beat the crowd inside.

"Nancy! It's terrible ... I don't know how it happened ..." Brenda says, running up to me.

"Brenda, take it easy. What happened?" I ask as I hear screaming in the distance.

"Gone! It's gone! Where is the first edition of *The Mystery at Lilac Inn?*" Dolly is screaming and walking right behind Brenda.

"That's what I was trying to tell you, Nancy! The book was there when we all ran out to the porch to see the northern lights, and now ... it's gone!" Brenda says.

"Dolly, please calm down! There must be a logical explanation for the book. Someone probably placed it somewhere for safekeeping. Okay, Piper? Maxine? Gail? Marlene? Do you know where it is?" I ask.

Oh, please, let that be the case. They are all shaking their heads no, and my stomach is feeling sick. I have to do something fast. This whole thing is turning into a disaster!

"Dolly and Perry, I'll address this shortly, but first, I have to take care of this crowd," I say, heading back through the lobby, up the stairs and down the hall to the Grand Ballroom.

At least Dolly regained her composure and stopped yelling. Thankfully, Katherine doesn't seem to be around. I think she excused herself when everyone went out to the porch. A saving grace in this fiasco.

Rushing back up to the microphone, I say as calmly as I can, "Ladies and gentlemen. We've had quite the evening, haven't we? Seems the limited-edition book we introduced has been misplaced. If any of you have information about it, please see me. But now, moving on. Remember that scavenger hunt sheet we handed out at the very beginning? Well, for the rest of the evening, we're going to give you a little head start on filling out your sheet. And then get a good night's sleep so you can finish it in the morning with all the outside clues. Feel free to visit the different booths and have fun talking about everything Nancy Drew!"

The crowd seems happy to entertain themselves while some head back outside to see if the lights are still there. Oh, great. Here comes the entourage, like a swarm of bees all talking at once.

"Listen, everyone, let's take this off the main floor, please. Follow me to the greenroom," I say.

At least they listened and don't cause another scene. Even as we settle into the room, I don't know what to say to them.

"Nancy. This is very serious. This was a rare first edition and we can't even put a dollar value on it. It appears that none of your assistants know where it is. I'm assuming it has been stolen. Someone took advantage of the room being empty, obviously, and stole it when we were all out on the porch," Perry says.

"Do you have some type of insurance? If so, and I hope you do, you should contact them right away," Dolly says.

"Yes, I have event liability insurance, but I don't think it covers this type of thing. There was no mention of the book in my forms, so I doubt it's something I could put in a claim for. I'm sorry it was taken, but surely you can't hold me responsible.

I didn't give you any guarantees of safety when you offered to let us display it," I say.

"I remember you saying you *would* keep it safe. If this book doesn't turn up, you will owe us not only for the book, but we will be withholding any further investment on your behalf, including the final payment.," Perry says.

"We need that payment! We've done well, and I need you to make that payment," I say.

"You can be assured that our lawyers will be contacting you, and we will be suing you for everything you and your husband have. We simply will not stand to be treated this way!" Dolly says with such anger, she's spitting while shouting her words.

Carrie, Larry, and Sherrie are all spouting threatening words too, getting uncomfortably close.

"Back off!"

Turning around, I'm so happy to see Ned in the doorway coming towards them. His presence seems to break the mood of whatever they had in mind, at least for the moment.

"We have appointments off the island we can't cancel, but we will be back at the end of the convention. You had better have your ducks in a row and have our book back or be ready to fully compensate us. There's no need for police at this point. We will be gracious and give you some time. Be warned! You don't mess around with the Masons as you will soon find out," Dolly says, turning and gesturing for the rest of them to follow her.

Her motley crew and a trail of sequins finally leave.

"Thank you, Ned. I think you just saved me from something. How long have you been standing there?" I ask.

"Long enough to wonder why you've been lying to me this whole time."

CHAPTER TWENTY-TWO

"So, you heard?" I ask.

"I heard the word 'sue' and 'last payment' which means *you* must be the financial backing behind this convention. It doesn't take a Nancy Drew investigation to figure out you're liable and you've put me in jeopardy too. Not only me, but our home, and what I leave my children. Is that how you got the backing? You forged my signature?" Ned asks.

I can hear in his voice he's trying to remain calm because we're not home, but it seems to be taking every ounce of self-control he has.

"Yes. It's how I got it done," I say.

"After I specifically told you not to! And all these months, you've kept up this charade. And now, with the stolen book, it's even worse. You put our future into the hands of that looney-toon couple with a woman who sheds sequins and a guy who looks like a reject from *Lifestyles of the Rich and Famous.*"

"You might as well know the whole truth. It's not just the book. They are the angel investors who backed the loan. I didn't know that until they showed up here. I hadn't met them ahead of time."

"Those people? *They're* rich enough to be angel investors? More like devil investors. You fit right in with them when it comes to deceit. Tell me everything, truthfully this time," Ned says.

And I do. I tell him about Penny, the loan, and how we would be okay financially if they had made the last payment as planned. The loan was based on future convention income, and now that won't be a possibility. We were barely making it with the loan and the agreement.

"Listen. I know it's not much help, but maybe we can still fix this. All us ladies are well-versed in solving mysteries thanks to Nancy Drew. We need to put our heads together and figure out who took the rare book. I also need to find out how Maxwell Powers is doing. I hope he is okay. Then, if we can find the book, and you sign a loan to finish the last payment in a traditional way, it will all be fine. I will pay back every cent. I swear I will. I'll get a job; I'll do whatever it takes to earn the money back. You won't lose a cent in the long run," I say.

"As mad as I am, I'm not a fan of thinking about my wife in jail for fraud. But forgive you? I'm not sure about that. This is so like you, Nancy! You take on these huge projects, doing things you've never done before. Why do you think you would know how to run a convention? You're so maddening sometimes! We will figure something out, but, yes, not having to pay for an old book on top of everything else would be a good start."

"Thank you, Ned. I am sorry. I wouldn't blame you if this is the final thing that breaks us up. I would get it," I say, bowing my head.

I don't want to look at his face.

"I don't know, Nancy. I don't. Right now, let's just get through this and try to get a good outcome."

"Sorry to interrupt ..."

Cam in the doorway startles us.

"Piper was looking for you with some questions, and I told her I would scout you out," Cam says with a smile until he sees our faces. "Is everything okay? I know the book missing is a kick in the pants, but we will find it. It can't have gone too far."

I turn to look at Ned and shrug. I'm not sure what to think anymore.

"You better go. I'll see you when I see you, I guess," Ned says as he passes Cam and heads out the door.

"Are you okay?" Cam asks, turning to me.

"There's a lot going on. I've been caught in some lies, and there are so many awful things happening," I say.

"Is there anything Piper and I can do?"

"If you can keep an eye on Ned, that would be good. I don't know if he's coming back to the convention or staying home. I have too much to do to chase him down."

"Absolutely, I can do that. Let me know how I can help in any way," Cam says.

"I better get back to my committee and see where we all are. Thanks, Cam. I need all the help I can get," I say.

"We've been praying already, Nancy. This can work out. Wait and see what God will do," he says.

"Oh, I hope so. Thanks again," I say, heading out the door to find my team.

I see Piper with the girls at the information table, all huddled together.

"Hi, gals. I'm so sorry I was absent for a minute. It's been a day to say the least," I say.

"How are you holding up?" Marlene asks.

"Anyone bring the book back by any chance?" I ask.

"Unfortunately, no. It's still missing. On the bright side, everyone is still having a good time with the various activities. What can we do to help?" Brenda asks.

"Here's what I think. We have all grown up with Nancy Drew, and this is our chance to put our sleuthing credentials to the real test. The question now is: can we figure out who took the book?"

"Yes! Yes, we can do it, especially because we've all been

praying for guidance and wisdom. God cares about the number of hairs on our heads, so He cares about this missing book," Sister Mary Margaret says.

"Well, it can't hurt," I say. "I also need to come clean about something else. My husband just found out and confronted me about the fact that I am the one who put up the financing for this convention. I've been hiding it from him all this time. He thought someone else was doing the financing. That's why I was so insistent you keep everything confidential."

They all look at me wide-eyed. No one seems to want to speak.

"I worked with an acquaintance of mine I know in Traverse City. You may or may not have picked up on the fact that the Masons revealed themselves to be those investors ... yes ... the very same people who brought the rare copy of *The Mystery at Lilac Inn,*" I say.

"Oh, no. So, they are super upset about the book, but also as your investors ..." Gail adds trailing off.

"Yes, they are upset about everything, and I was counting on them for one more payment. We haven't quite made enough after expenses to do it without them. They were committed to making their money back in future conventions, taking the chance this one would be successful and profitable. As you can imagine, they aren't going to be very willing to keep up the relationship. Here's something else they don't know, but it can land me in hot water. I falsified Ned's signature. I could get in trouble for that too. They can come after me and my husband's finances, including our home," I say. "Ned was right. What business did I have heading up a Nancy Drew convention when I've never even been to one? I love her books, but I don't know all this background information about her. It's becoming clear I know very little."

"Wow, Nancy. You weren't kidding when you said you've had a day," Piper says, putting her arm around me.

"Listen, girls. I wouldn't blame you if every one of you were so disgusted with me that you took off and never looked back. I would appreciate you staying until the end of the convention. None of you had anything to do with this, so you are safe from any accusations. That I am sure of," I say.

"I think I can speak for all of us when I say we are here for you. Let us help you work through this. And we will be praying and trying to understand what the answers are to make this have a good outcome," Piper says.

"Thank you. I don't deserve it, but it means so much to have you helping me. I think we should all shut down for the evening. Keep notes as ideas come to you about what might be happening. Tomorrow, after breakfast when the attendees are all in their breakout sessions, let's meet in the greenroom. We can keep an eye on the convention, and work out who might have had the means, motive, and opportunity to commit this crime. I do believe by working together, we can get further than me trying to figure this out alone, even if my name is Nancy," I say. "Did we get any word on Maxwell Powers? Is he going to be okay?"

"I'm keeping up on his condition. The hospital is keeping me posted. He's still not responding well, and they are doing more tests. It sounds to me like either this is a very bad flu, or something else is going on. I'm hoping we'll know more tomorrow," Maxine says.

"Yes, please. The minute you know something, let me know. I feel so bad. Just one more fiasco from the day," I say.

"At least the attendees seem satisfied with everything. All the comments I've overheard have been positive. Of course, they are concerned for Maxwell, but the tidbits he did give are things they want to explore," Gail says.

"Okay ladies. We have our marching orders. Everyone work with their roommate tonight and try to figure out what happened to the book. Then tomorrow, after we get everyone where they need to be, we'll work together. Say your prayers and put on your thinking caps. We have a crime to solve!" Piper says.

With murmurings of agreement, they all head toward their

rooms. I should do the same, but I have a stop to make. Somewhere that I've gone to think in the past. I know it's dark. I know I should go to bed. But there's no way I can get much sleep. I know where to go.

CHAPTER TWENTY-THREE

*G*rabbing my sweater and the flashlight out of my satchel, I go through the main parlor, across the porch, and down the stairs into the lawn and garden area of the Grand grounds. The grass is cold and wet on my ankles, but I don't care.

Oh, how much easier things were at our Fourth of July celebration on this very lawn, watching fireworks and feeling happy with Ned. That was the first time Cam and Piper showed us the little secret beyond the pool—the Grand Labyrinth—nestled in a tiny, wooded area below the Grand. This prayer circle designed every year by Cam has become my place of solace, even though I'm not one of those "prayers." Most times I've snuck in here, it's been empty, the best kept secret on the Grand's grounds. I couldn't believe it when Cam and Piper told us this is where they had their wedding! This little spot of earth filled with the labyrinth pattern made of stones and mounded dirt still has some of the flowers peeking through that have lasted through the season. It feels more sacred than any church I've ever visited. Ever since the Fourth, this is where I come to think, get centered, and try to figure things out.

Ah, to be back on that day in July. Now everything is one big mess. I wouldn't blame Ned if he kicked me out of his life and demanded the money back for every cent we are going to lose.

Going past the pool and around the trees, I see the opening. I know if I can get there and sit on the bench in front of the labyrinth, I can think more clearly. Something will come to me. It may all make sense. There, my eyes are adjusted to the dark. I don't need this flashlight. Thank you, moon.

Wait! Someone is already in there. I hear voices, male voices. Oh man, maybe this wasn't such a good idea. Way to go, Nancy. A female out in the small woods alone, late at night. That's all I need for something else to happen. Ugh, I so wanted to be there tonight.

Hey! I know that voice. And the other voice, too. If I go slowly, I should be able to get closer but stay hidden in the bushes. I can hear them without them seeing me if I'm very careful.

I guess Cam took my plea seriously. It's Cam and Ned on the bench, talking quietly. Maybe this place meant something to Ned, too, after he visited. I've come this far; I might as well add eavesdropping to my list of loser qualities.

"I can't get over the fact she forged my signature. She takes on these grandiose projects with no training or background just because she likes something. Thank goodness we don't have a cat, or she'd have a cat convention next. I mean, with all of this it makes me wonder, what else has she done?" Ned asks.

Oh, great. Now all my girlfriends *and* Cam know the scoundrel side of me. Still, it's probably good Ned has someone to talk to.

"I agree she shouldn't have done it, but now that it's out there, she could use your support," Cam says.

"Support? For lying and putting our entire future in jeopardy?" Ned asks.

"It's done. Now we have to deal with the current situation.

I'm hoping all those ladies who have read so many Nancy Drew books will have some great detective skills to make sense of all this. Remember what we talked about, Ned? About giving your life to Jesus? This is a time you're going to need your Heavenly Father's love going through you to Nancy, to forgive her. There's a story in the Bible where one of Jesus' disciples, Peter, asks Him if we should forgive seven times. Jesus answers, seventy times seven. That's not an exact number; it means forgiveness should be limitless. That's how He forgives us when we are sorry. If Nancy is sorry, which she said she was, she needs your forgiveness," Cam says.

"I don't know if I can forgive her. I don't know if I want to be married to her anymore, if I can ever trust her again," Ned says.

Ouch. That really hurts. As many times as I wish he would have fallen off a cliff, it hurts my heart to hear him not want me.

"Forgiveness means you keep going, and you work through this. You can set boundaries about always telling each other the truth about finances. But, yes, it all begins with you forgiving her. And in our humanness, we don't see it. It's through our love for Jesus that we see the way to forgive others who harm us. I get it. It's not how you feel. We can't make these important decisions on feelings. In the long run, not forgiving Nancy will hurt you a lot more than it will hurt her. Have you read the Bible I gave you?" Cam asks.

Do Piper and Cam own stock in Bibles or something? They give them out like candy!

"I read in the book called John, like you told me. I've been thinking about it," Ned says quietly. "How do you and Piper get along so well?"

"Believe me. We aren't perfect. There's a verse that says a triple braided cord is not easily broken. That's what we have at the basis of our marriage, that triple cord. It's Piper, me, and Jesus and the promises we made right here in this spot at our wedding. It makes all the difference. We still get short-tempered with each other, snippy, and grouchy sometimes. It mostly happens when the 'old me' is in charge. When I look at the big picture, I think marriages that truly work are accountable to Jesus, not to themselves. Left to ourselves, we humans can be greedy and selfish," Cam says. "I know I sure can."

"I won't ever say what she did was right, but it's true. I didn't give her much support about how she could follow this passion to have this convention. I am thinking about that verse in John about God loving the world so much that He sent His Son to die for anyone who believes," Ned says.

"That's the one. And that 'anyone' is you, and Nancy, and me, and Piper ... and you get the picture," Cam says.

"I'm trying to get there. I'll keep reading. I'll keep praying," Ned says.

Ned prays? Ned reads the Bible? What's next? Ned will go to church? Please. Cam's words are nice, but he doesn't live with Ned and see what I see. But then, no one has seen the real Nancy either. I don't know. Be honest, Ned. You are no saint!

"I should get going. I've been up since dawn and there's more to do this weekend. You should get some sleep, too. Let's pray, Ned. Would that be okay?" Cam asks.

"I'm not going to say no. I need something," Ned says.

"Dear Lord, please continue to show yourself to Ned and Nancy. Please help us with this situation regarding the stolen book, the finances, and please be with Mr. Powers, that he will be okay. Give all those ladies wisdom for the rest of the convention, give them strength, and help them all to go to You for whatever they need. Thank you for forgiving us. Give Ned a new love for Nancy and help him forgive. Help him to know You. We ask it in Jesus' name, Amen."

"Amen. Thanks, Cam," Ned says as they stand and start to head toward the opening of the labyrinth.

"Happy to help, Ned. Weren't those northern lights fantastic?"

Their voices are trailing away, and I feel safe enough to slip out of the woods and take my place on the bench next to the labyrinth path. Deep breaths Nancy. At the end of this weekend, will I have a husband, a home, or any answers? Okay God. If you're real, this would be a perfect time for you to show up. I don't deserve it, but could you help a girl out here?

CHAPTER TWENTY-FOUR

"*I*'m waiting for a call from the hospital to see how Maxwell is doing. Last I heard, he was still out of it, and they were running tests. I hope to get a message soon that I can call back and check up on him, poor guy. He seemed like he had such interesting news ... I mean, saying Carolyn Keene was a made-up name, she didn't actually write the books. That's new to me," Maxine says.

"I love reading Nancy Drew, but I can't keep up with these historians for sure. I'm happy to report the posters are selling like hotcakes, especially the one with multiple Nancy Drew covers," Brenda says. "I can't wait to see the people's faces when we serve cake at the afternoon tea. The cakes have been made to look like the book covers of many of the books, and they are fabulous! It will be a great ending to the convention."

"I hope you all know how much I appreciate you. You've kept everything running so smoothly," I say. "And hearing the merch is selling is really good news."

"The breakout sessions are going as planned and there are plenty of participants at each one. We've got people making bookmarks, listening to the local librarian's presentation, and playing Nancy Drew bingo. All the church and library volunteers have everything under control so we can meet," Gail says. "We couldn't have done it without their help."

Tucked inside the greenroom next to the stage, I can see we are all in sleuthing mode. Good. I need help.

"So, what do we know? Let's think like Nancy Drew with some Agatha Christie thrown in and solve this crime! Someone had to have means, motive, and opportunity. Let's cross off opportunity right away. I think absolutely everyone was out on the porch watching the northern lights, so everyone had the opportunity to sneak back in here and take the book," I say.

"I should have taken the book with me! I still feel so bad that I got caught up in the excitement to get out on the porch and see the lights. I'm so sorry," Brenda says.

"Brenda, no one blames you. Really, I should have stayed behind and kept an eye on things. I guess none of us wanted to think anyone here would actually do anything like that, so we were all a bit naïve. Please, don't feel bad or we will all feel bad that you are sad! If that makes sense!" I say.

Everyone murmurs their agreement.

"I even went as far as to suspect Ned, because he's the one who made the call for everyone to head to the porch," I say.

"Ned? Your husband? Come on, Nancy," Gail says.

"I know that sounds silly, but we haven't seen eye-to-eye on this convention. It's been rough going at our house. I wondered if he was trying to teach me a lesson. Even saying it out loud, I know he wouldn't do that," I say.

"I don't think he would either," Piper adds. "Even if times are hard, Ned loves you."

"That's a thought for another day. Let's talk about motive. I guess there are two theories. Someone attending collects rare Nancy Drew editions and they don't have *The Mystery at Lilac Inn*. Or someone attending thinks it's valuable, steals it, and plans on selling it," I say.

"How much is it worth? Do we know?" Sister Mary Margaret asks.

"I don't. The past few days I'm learning there's tons I don't know about Nancy Drew. I thought loving the books was enough to throw a convention. Oh, so dumb. Before I nixed the budget, did you find out much about first editions, Brenda?" I ask.

"Nancy don't be so hard on yourself. The regular convention is going fine. We couldn't know there would be a robbery. Anyway, I talked to one of the visiting librarians last night. She helped me understand more about what makes a Nancy Drew book valuable. According to her, there are only three Nancy Drew books that are first edition and rarer. They are *The Secret of the Old Clock*, First Edition—the inaugural book. *The Whispering Statue*, Signed, First Edition, and *The Mystery at the Moss-Covered Mansion*, Signed, First Edition. I found out you need to look under the original 30s and 40s dust jackets and make sure it's a blue hardcover with orange embossed writing. Those are worth the most collectively out of any printings in the series. It also seems that those with dust jackets are worth more. She was very excited to see the book we had as a rare first edition, but then, you know, it went missing."

"That's interesting. You know, I didn't look at the book that closely with all the million things going on, but I think it was signed by Carolyn Keene. Yes, I think it was. So, maybe that's what made this one so rare?" I ask.

"Could this be the only one with that signature? Or did one of the ghostwriters sign the name Carolyn Keene? It's all a bit confusing now that we know there was no actual Carolyn Keene according to Maxwell," Sister Mary Margaret says.

"Maxine, when you get to talk to Maxwell, which I hope you do, ask him the value of *The Mystery at Lilac Inn*, with a dust cover, signed by Carolyn Keene. Try to get a ballpark if you can. Even if we don't find the book, I'll have some idea of what I would need to pay the Bensons to compensate for the loss," I say.

"I'll make it a priority for sure," Maxine says.

"They got mad so quickly and flew off the handle. I mean, the book could still turn up. As angel investors, I wouldn't think they would be short on money, meaning the actual value of the book can't be something that is a huge amount in *their* world. Maybe they were more upset because of sentimental value, or because it was signed?" Sister Mary Margaret asks.

"And they took off. They left firm instructions not to call the police which is a little odd too," I say. "I wasn't sure about calling the police, but if we can settle this ourselves, it will be much easier."

"Brenda, did you take a good look around the plexiglass box after the book was taken?" Sister Mary Margaret asks.

"No, not really. I probably should have. Ugh, that's not very Nancy Drew of me!" Brenda says.

"I'll go with you when our meeting is done. Let's look extra closely. We might find something. I don't think dusting for fingerprints would do any good, even if we could. Surely the thief wore gloves. But it can't hurt to take a closer look," Sister says.

"That is a good idea, and I didn't think of it either," I say. "When it comes to opportunity, everyone is a suspect. What if it isn't even one of our attendees?"

"You're right. We aren't the only people in the hotel. There are other guests, and people stopping in to see the Grand. Someone could have scoped out the convention out of nosiness, seen the book was highlighted, known it was valuable, and waited for a chance to steal it. Although ... wouldn't other things be missing, too? As far as I could tell, everything else is still here," Marlene says.

"Good point," Piper says. "Someone having means ... that's also everyone. Everyone was capable of taking the book with the room empty. Who knew we would need security guards at our little convention. What's the world coming to?"

"So, this crime comes down to motive. Was the book theft premeditated or a spur-of-the moment snatch?" Gail asks.

"Seems like snatching! Ugh! I don't know … trying to solve this crime may be like a needle in the haystack. Remember in *The Clue of the Crossword Cipher* when the clue was carved on a wooden plaque that was so old, most of the crossword cipher was obliterated? No matter how hopeless it looked, Nancy and the gang didn't give up. They kept at it. That's what we have to do," I say trying to convince myself as much as them.

"You're right. We have to keep at it," Piper says. "Just so you know, I'm willing to pitch in to help pay for whatever I can. You don't need to shoulder this burden alone, Nancy."

"I want to help too," Marlene says.

I feel my eyes filling with tears as each lady says they will help financially.

"You ladies floor me once again. Thank you. No one is pitching in anything, but your heartfelt encouragement is priceless to me," I say, wiping away tears.

"You're going to get us all crying!" Maxine says.

"Honestly, I've never had such faithful friends in my life. What would I do without all of you?" I ask.

"Nancy, would you mind if we stopped and just said a prayer? There's a verse in the book of James that talks about what to do if you don't know what to do. It's James 1:5 'If any of you lacks wisdom, you should ask God, who gives generously to all without finding fault, and it will be given to you,' Sister says. "I have it memorized because, well, I am short on wisdom often. And why rely on just me when God has promised to guide me and to do it generously! I mean, that's a promise I want in my life!"

"Hey, I'll take wisdom right now. I'm backed into a corner, and I don't have the answer on how to solve all of this," I say.

"Sister's right. There's no amount of brainstorming on our own that can add up to getting some Holy Spirit help as to what to do and where to look. I think saying a prayer is exactly what we need right now," Piper says.

As they all bow their heads, I don't. I look at them. Each one asks for that generous wisdom Sister Mary Margaret talked about. Looking at their faces I see authentic faith. These people really believe in a God who affects their everyday life. They talk to Him like we talk to each other. My heart is feeling, well, something. Something bigger than me. Something hopeful. Something ...

CRASH!

The familiar voice outside the door makes my heart sink.

"Well, you shouldn't have a cart sitting right there. It's a safety hazard! Please get this cleaned up right now. I wouldn't have run into it and made such a mess if it had been cleaned up properly."

Oh, great. Katherine Sims-Dubois has been outside our thin little greenroom door, and I wonder how long she's been listening. And why didn't we hear the swishing of her skirt when we were quietly praying?

CHAPTER TWENTY-FIVE

Seated closest to the door, Marlene grabs the handle and opens it quickly. We all get to see a flustered Katherine and the remnants of the cart filled with glasses crashed around her, including red juice that has sprayed across her skirt.

"Look at me! I should think you'd be more careful than to allow a cart filled with glasses of juice to be placed so close to a door!" she says, glaring at all of us.

Cart sounds more like "cot" coming out of her mouth.

"I'm so sorry. Thank you so much for cleaning this up," I say to the gentleman cleaning up the shattered glass and wiping up the juice.

"No problem, milady," he says while quickly taking care of the spills and mess.

"Can we help you, Katherine? How long have you been waiting to talk with us?" I ask.

"Longer than I should have had to, that's for sure," she says. "Perhaps you'd like to pay for the dry-cleaning bill to get this juice out of my skirt?"

What's on her skirt this time? Oh, yes. It's the lady slipper skirt I saw in the spring. My goodness, she does wear something twice.

"Are those lady slippers on your skirt, Katherine?" Maxine asks, probably trying to change the subject and calm her down. "They are so beautiful here on the island in the spring. Did you know the Ojibwe people named the flower *ma-ki-sin waa-big-waan*, which means the moccasin flower. They have a story about a young maiden named Running Flower who runs through the forest to save the people of her village. The tale—"

"Oh, for Pete's sake. Yes, they are lady slippers, and yes, of course I know everything there is to know about any tale that has ever happened on this island. You don't get to be the town chairwoman and have your ancestry tied to the very core of a place without knowing everything," Katherine sputters.

With her flushed face and embarrassment, I don't think she did hear much, or she would be smarmily spouting something at me.

"And who are you, Miss …. Miss … storyteller?" Katherine asks.

"I'm Maxine. We've met before, Katherine," Maxine says.

"Well, I can't be expected to remember every little person … uh … I mean … the names of all the people I meet. Anyway, you are the one I'm looking for. I was at the main desk when a message came in for you and I said I would pass it along. Maxwell Powers is ready for a phone call. There. That's the thanks I get for doing my civic duty and delivering a message," Katherine says.

"Oh, good. Are we done here, Nancy?" Maxine asks, turning to me. "I'd like to follow up right away."

"Yes, and please let me know how he is doing. And get some answers if you can," I say as she rushes out the door.

"Can we help you with something else, Katherine?" I ask.

"Well, as it's the last day of this gathering, I'm sure you need me to make some closing remarks to the attendees," she says.

"No. We have that all covered. Thank you, we won't be

needing your services. You had better get some club soda on that skirt. That juice is going to leave a stain," I say as I close the door in her face. "And be careful before someone drops a house on you, too," I say softly so only they can hear.

For once in my life, I have the perfect line at the perfect time.

Of course, these Nancy Drew loving gals get *The Wizard of Oz* reference and burst out laughing. It feels good to lighten the load a moment with laughter. When she doesn't feel like a thorn in your side, Katherine is always good for a little comic relief. She and the Masons could be in the next issue of *Vogue*. Uh ... maybe not.

"I'm so glad we are going to hear how Maxwell is doing and get some more facts. I think I need to make a phone call too. My problems will be here later. Right now, let's get back out there and make sure the attendees have a memorable ending to their experience. That will be our focus. Thanks again for everything you're doing," I say.

I love every single hug I get as they head out. These girls have saved my life. I hope we can stay close after the convention. Okay. What's next. Oh, yes. Head to the phone booths outside the Grand Ballroom and make a call.

Oh great. There she is once again—Katherine. I wish she would leave. And, perfect. She has Ned cornered and is touching her hair, his arm, and flirting up a storm. I guess she wasn't too concerned about the juice stain after all. I simply don't have time to wonder about that at this moment. Maybe he's already looking around and thinking about throwing me out. Yeah, he sees me. And he still keeps talking to her. Telling.

I should have called Penny sooner. Hanging up the phone, I can't stop thinking about what she told me. What was it ... such financial mumbo jumbo. *If a preset performance metric isn't met, the investment becomes a loan.* So, that's not so bad. It becomes a loan. Even if Ned won't help, I can pay for a loan somehow. I'll have to move back to Traverse City and get a job. That's what I'll do.

Then she said something about falsification of business records or acting fraudulently ... well. I guess signing someone else's name could be considered fraudulent in some circles. Oh, Ned. If only you would go along with this for a short time until I get out of this jam. Then I would leave you alone. I wonder—oh, he's not talking to Swishy-Swishy anymore. Now she's regaling her juice incident to one of her minions.

Where did Ned go? Is he simply going to ignore me? Maybe I can find him in the lobby.

Wow! The hotel is busy today. With everything going on, I didn't notice all the other people visiting. Wait, I see him. Who is he flirting with now? Really Ned? Now you're flirting with Sister Mary Margaret? Hmmmm ... if I quietly tip toe over here behind this corner and big fern I can hear them, but they can't see me. This might be interesting to see how he makes a move on a nun! I know what my next profession will be: professional eavesdropper.

"There's only one way forward, Ned. And that's forgiveness," Sister Mary Margaret says.

"Why should I forgive her? She's put our whole future in jeopardy. I specifically told her I didn't want to do the money part of the convention. She went ahead and did it anyway," Ned says.

Yeah, Ned. I did it anyway because you should have backed me up and not made me go behind your back. I should jump in this conversation and defend myself, but where would that get me? What's up with you, Ned? Do you feel the need to tell everyone how bad I am?

"In the short-term, you probably just want to be right, and make her understand how angry you are. But look at the big picture. You asked Nancy to marry you for a reason. That person is still there. Are you willing to give up your future over this one small chapter in your story?" Sister asks Ned.

"I can't get past this moment. Part of me knows that's a dumb way to look at things," Ned says quietly.

Speak up Ned, I'm trying to hear this conversation!

"I don't know if you are a man of faith, but we are told in the Bible to forgive. The person we hurt the most when we don't forgive ends up being ourselves. And if Jesus can forgive us, we can forgive others," Sister says. "That's not just for those of us considered religious by the world. If you look at the big picture once again, you'll see the wisdom in what Jesus told us to do," Sister says. "I don't think it's a coincidence we sat down in these chairs next to each other. I believe this is a message you need to hear and take to heart."

"You know who you sound like?" Ned asks.

"Who?" Sister asks.

"Cam. He's been talking to me about Jesus, and he said the same thing. I don't know. I just don't know," Ned says.

"What is holding you back? Have you prayed to have a relationship with Jesus?" Sister asks.

"I think I'm getting closer to wanting to do that," Ned says.

I've got to put a stop to this. That's all I need, "religious Ned" on top of all his other quirks. I know. I'll make it look like I tripped and at the same time I'll be able to leap in front of them.

"Oh, there you are, Ned. Hi, Sister Mary Margaret. I was looking for Ned, and there he is. Do you mind if I steal him away for a minute?" I ask.

"Not at all. Ned, feel free to speak to Cam. Your authentic life story awaits!" she says. "I'll go see if Piper needs help. Oh, Nancy. I didn't get to see you, but when Brenda and I were looking around the plexiglass case, we didn't find much. Only two small sequins next to the box. That was it. See you guys."

Sequins? Hmmm. As we watch her leave, we have a moment of staring at each other.

"Well, you said you were looking for me?" Ned says.

I'm not hearing forgiveness in that tone. Maybe he was telling her what he thought she wanted to hear. That sounds more like Ned.

"Yes. I wanted to make sure you were okay. I mean, I'm still trying to figure out who took the book. Things could all work out fine," I say, looking at his face for a clue he's going to cooperate with me in any way.

"Of course you would like me to forget it. After all, you don't want me to be the one who makes it clear that you fraudulently signed my name. That would be a much bigger problem, wouldn't it?"

"Yes. You would have to visit me in jail, and I hope you would at least bake a cake with a file in it!"

Ha! I saw a corner of a smile.

"Honestly, I'm too mixed up to know what I think. What can I do to help you right now? Let's concentrate on that," Ned says.

"Maybe watch yourself around Katherine Sims-Dubois," I say, lowering my voice, so people around won't hear.

"Really, Nancy? What am I supposed to do? Run the other way when she approaches me?" Ned asks. "It's a small town. We are bound to run into one another."

"Yes, I think any husband would think it wise to avoid someone like that. She always seems to be stroking your arm or something," I say.

"Oh, and that bothers you if someone else doesn't think I'm totally repulsive?" Ned asks.

"I don't think that. Give me a break. There's too much going on to be talking about this," I say.

"I agree. So, what's next?" he asks.

"I have some unanswered questions, and I need to make a phone call. Something is eating at me, and I hope it will steer me into some answers."

"So, what's holding you back? Make that phone call," he says. "I'll go see if any of your committee girls need help with anything and if they don't, I'll see what Cam is up to."

"You're really getting close to Cam, aren't you?" I ask.

"Just like you're close to Piper," he says.

"There's probably some things we can learn from them. They're a lot younger, and we are the ones who need to observe them. I mean, the whole God thing," I say, looking for his reaction.

"Yes, the God thing. It seems to work for them. What we have going on doesn't seem to be working for us. Maybe it is time to turn to someone other than our own ideas. Cam gave me a Bible," he says.

"Did you read it?"

"A little. I started with a book called John, at Cam's suggestion," he says.

"Nancy! I've been looking everywhere for you!" Maxine says rushing up to us. "Oh. Hi, Ned. Sorry to interrupt but Nancy! Maxwell has taken a turn for the better. He's awake, eating, and he said it's important to get this message to you."

"What did he say?" I ask.

"He said ..." Before Maxine can say another word, there they are, surrounding us. The Masons and their entourage all look like cheshire cats who just had a bowl of cream.

CHAPTER TWENTY-SIX

"*N*ancy, we've consulted with our lawyer, and we have a specific way we want this to go. We want you to pay us now, and then you can get reimbursed with the insurance policy you have for the convention. We know through our appraisal sources the book is worth $10,000, so we will settle for $5,000 *if* you comply with our requests. We want to avoid all the publicity and dragging our good name through the mud, which is why we don't want the police involved. It can be a simple matter," Perry Mason says.

"I see. Why not wait for the insurance money if it's worth that much?" I ask.

"It's not only the money, but also the principle. Obviously, as people with the means to be angel investors, we are not short on cash. However, we do feel you need to be held responsible in some way for what was allowed to happen here," Dolly says.

Her troop all nods in agreement.

"Now, should you choose to go a different direction, then the price will keep going up. You can repay us for the book and for the pain and suffering we are enduring. Our lawyer was quite clear that we would have no trouble winning this type of lawsuit," Perry says.

Thankfully, it's been an empty lobby up until this point, but more people are starting to show up.

"Listen, we don't need to be making a scene here. Let's move this into the greenroom by the stage. Please all go there, and I'll see about having your money ready. I don't want the police involved either. There's no need for any of that. If you're hungry or thirsty, I'm sure it's been restocked with beverages and treats. Go there and wait," I say. "Ned, please escort everyone to the greenroom. I'll be there shortly."

Ned knows by the tone of my voice he should do what I asked.

"Let's go, folks. Soon you'll have a check so we can put this matter behind us. As her husband, she has my full backing," he says.

I see the soft wink as he ushers them toward the room.

"Oh, I want more of those crackers that look like little fish!" Larry says as they are leaving.

Larry, Carrie, and Sherry feel the need to discuss their cracker preferences as they follow Ned.

"Finally. Now I can tell you what Maxwell said you should know. I also found out something else at the check-in desk," Maxine says.

"Whisper it in my ear. There's too many people around now. I think I already know what you are going to say." I say.

As Maxine whispers her news in my ear, things are finally making sense.

"Go get all the gals and get them to the greenroom too. The volunteers can handle things for a minute or two. I'm going to make two quick phone calls, and I'll join you there," I say.

Watching Maxine leave, I already know what I'm going to find out. Suddenly, everything is crystal clear.

∼

*H*anging up the phone, I can't believe I've been so naïve. Mistake after mistake was made, by me. I have apologies to make to so many people. Heading for the greenroom, some truth is finally going to come out, and it's about time. I don't have all the answers, but I have enough to put out this fire.

As I enter the greenroom, everyone turns to look at me.

"So, let's get this finished. Do you have the check?" Dolly asks.

"I don't. And I won't be giving you a check. In fact, I'll be contacting a lawyer to see what you can be sued for because of what you've just done. Maybe I'll even contact the police. It all depends on what you have to say."

CHAPTER TWENTY-SEVEN

"*P*reposterous! Who do you think you are? We invest in your convention, and you treat us like this? Fine! It's no longer $5,000, it's now $10,000 and probably going higher," Dolly screams at me.

"Well, let's break it down. First of all: the book. The book you mentioned is a rare first edition signed by Carolyn Keene. You don't know it, but Maxwell is doing fine, and he's talking. Too bad he had to leave feeling sick, because if he had stayed, he would have told us right away *The Mystery at Lilac Inn* isn't that rare. There are lots of copies circulating, something I simply didn't do enough research to know. That's my fault," I say.

"Well, it was presented to us as rare and worth tons of money," Perry says. "How were we to know any differently?"

"He also said Carolyn Keene didn't sign the books. In fact, all the books were written by ghostwriters whose names we are just now starting to understand. Carolyn Keene is not a real person. Anything signed which is rare and worth money would be signed by one of the ghostwriters, using their real names. Trying to pass off a book signed by Carolyn Keene was your first mistake," I say.

"Well, I never!" Dolly says.

"I think you probably have, Dolly. My quick phone call to my friend in charge of the angel investor loan also made things very clear. There are no investors by the names of Dolly and Perry Mason. You are frauds, trying to fraudulently get money from our committee," I say.

"Ridiculous!" Perry yells.

"You are grifters who pull off stunts if you think there's money involved for you. And you were most likely set up by a grifter I used to have in my life. I'm sure he was going to get a cut of your earnings," I say.

"Nancy? Your ..." Ned asks.

"Yes, Ned. My ex-husband has pulled a fast one because of the information he got from my friend Penny who was involved with my loan. They dated for a brief time, which is where he got the information to do this—all to mess with me. It's what he loved to do when we were married, and what he has continued to do sporadically. He put you up to this, didn't he?" I ask.

"Absurd!" Dolly shouts.

"Oh, enough!" Sherrie says. "Yes, it *was* Phillip. We were all in a local theatre troupe together and he said he knew how we could have some fun and make a quick buck. Plus, we owed him one. He's half blackmailing us, too, for a job we pulled. He's always threatened to go to the authorities. This seemed an easy way to appease him and make some cash while having a fun vacation."

"Shut up, Sherrie!" Dolly says.

"You shut up, Dolly," Carrie says.

Might as well hear from the third minion.

"Hey, Larry. Do you have anything to add?" I ask.

"We didn't even get to stay at the Grand Hotel like he originally said!" Larry says.

"Oh, I know. That came out too when Maxine was talking to the check-in desk. None of you had these big appointments off the island. In fact, you were all staying in a cheap hotel in Mackinaw City and coming back on a ferry every day. And you didn't get to stay here at the Grand? Seems Phillip didn't fund your ruse very well, now did he? And Dolly, for your next adventure, think about the fact that high-end, sparkly clothing doesn't shed every two seconds. Maxine found out you left quite an impression on the ferry crew, who had to sweep up after you every night," I say.

"What do you expect from thrift shop clothes? Cheap creep Phillip. He's going to get his for this, believe me," Dolly says. "So, the gig is up. We all had a good laugh, and we'll be on our way."

"I don't think so Dolly, if that is your real name," I say. "There's a bigger issue, the question of who poisoned Maxwell's tea so he would get sick and not be able to call you out on your fake book. You must have panicked when you realized if he saw the book, he would be on to all of you. So you did something to keep him quiet. But poisoning someone? That is not just a 'gig.' That's a crime." I say. "Brenda, would you open the door and let the officers in, please?"

As Brenda opens the doors and the two Mackinac Island officers walk in, the jaws of the frauds drop.

"One of the phone calls I had to make was to our trusty Mackinac Island Police Department," I say.

"Please come with us, you five. You're headed directly to St. Ignace under suspicion for attempted murder," the taller officer says as the other officer starts to cuff each of them. "We've been in contact with the Traverse City Police, and we have a pretty good idea of what happened here."

Obscenities fly as they point fingers at each other while the officer reads their Miranda rights.

"What happened to innocent until proven guilty?" Perry screams.

"You can call your lawyers and take care of all the details when we get to St. Ignace to start the booking process," the tall officer says. "I know a back way to exit the hotel, so we don't cause as much of a ruckus. Let's go."

"Larry and Carrie did the poisoning!" Dolly shrieks.

"Sherrie did it!" Larry says, longingly looking at the goldfish crackers.

"Perry did it!" Carrie says trying to talk over Larry.

"Dolly did it!" Sherrie wailed.

"Shut up ... all of you! Are you idiots? We didn't poison anyone! They don't have proof ... no proof!" Perry says.

"It's pretty apparent one or all of you slipped into the green-room at some point and poisoned the pitcher of tea clearly marked for Maxwell only," I say. "One of you put rat poison in his tea. He's tested positive for thallium, a tasteless, fast way to poison someone. Thallium is easy to get if you purchase rat poison."

"We didn't fill up that iced tea pitcher. One of your people did," Larry says.

"No one from my team was in here after you guys were. And no one from my team was in on a ruse to get money. It was my team member Maxine who clearly labeled the tea pitcher with her handwriting. Why would she do that if she had something to hide?" I ask. "Officer, would you mind looking in Dolly's bag before you go? I think you'll find the missing Nancy Drew novel in question."

Grabbing her bag, the tall officer pulls out the book.

"It's not a crime to take back your own book!" Dolly sneers.

"It is if you act like it was stolen and try to get insurance money! Officer, if you would turn that book in for evidence, please. I think the investigators will be able to match the signature to the ultimate culprit of this crime," I say. "Please take them away, Officers."

As they leave, they continue to accuse each other, which has become almost comical.

"Whoa, Nancy. I guess all your Nancy Drew reading really paid off," Ned says.

"It was all of you once again. And the few weird things that have happened lately. Maxwell's message, finding out from Maxine they weren't staying here when they said they were … and ultimately—those stupid sequins! Once Sister told me they were in the plexiglass case, I knew Dolly was involved. Piper would not have set up a case and left a speck of dust, let alone sequins," I say.

"Very true. There were no sequins when the case was set up," Piper says.

"Thank God, you discovered it all. And poor Maxwell. Could he have died?" Sister Mary Margaret asks.

"Yes, he could have. I'm not taking the credit for this. Maxine, tell them what he said," I say.

"Maxwell is on the mend. I think the intent was always to sicken him, not kill him. It depends now on how much he wants to pursue charges against that crazy group. At least they will all be detained for now and the legal system will have to take its course. I bet you're right, Nancy. When they analyze that signature in *The Mystery at Lilac Inn*, it will match the mastermind behind this whole thing—your ex-husband Phillip," Maxine says. "I'll follow up to make sure that piece of the puzzle is thoroughly explored. Guess Phillip didn't read *The Clue of the Whistling Bagpipes*. Pity! Then he would have known you have to be careful where you put your autograph."

"Great observation, Maxine! What a whirlwind … all while a convention is happening at the same time. I think we better get out there. We've asked a lot of our volunteers, and they will need a break," Piper says.

"You're right, Piper. Thanks again, everyone. We'll regroup after the official closing of the convention. We've had enough excitement to last for a long time. How *did* Nancy do this in book after book?" I ask.

That got a much-needed laugh from everyone. As they all file out, I am wondering how Ned is feeling about everything.

"Ned, thank you for picking up on my cue. You could have

gone home and said, 'the heck with me' on this whole thing, but I appreciate you coming back and sticking with me through it all," I say.

He really surprised me.

"I wasn't going to. I wanted to throw your things out on the curb and teach you a lesson. But then Cam intervened. We had a good talk. He convinced me that I needed to forgive you and make things right. I was wavering again and then Sister Mary Margaret said the same thing. But ... uh... when it comes to making things right, I recently told Cam the truth about something else. I've come to realize if there's any hope for us, I need to tell you the truth, too," Ned says.

"The truth, about what? I'm afraid to hear what you have to say."

When he utters that name, my knees feel weak. Falling into the chair near me, this is a step too far.

CHAPTER TWENTY-EIGHT

"So, you *have* been seeing her? You've been seeing the person I can't stand most on this island—Katherine Sims-Dubois! I suspected you, but deep down, I thought ... no, he would never stoop that low!" I say.

"We have *both* stooped low in our efforts to hurt each other and get revenge."

"Why her? She's a horrible person! Anyone but her!"

"To be clear, nothing really happened. It was flirting and giving her a little too much attention, innocent attention, mind you. Yes, I agree that crosses the line for a married man, but nothing physical happened. I want you to know that," Ned says.

"*Yet*, you mean. Nothing happened yet, because you what, felt sorry for me with all this convention mayhem? Is that it? If the convention had gone fine, you would have pursued her more. Is that true?"

"Yes. No! I don't know! I don't even like her that much. I just saw her as a way to get back at you for all the neglect I've felt in this marriage for the past year."

"Right back at you, buddy boy! You don't care about anything that is important to me. It's all about *your* woodshop, *your* kids, *your* money. Anything I wanted to do was put on the back burner. There was nothing for *your* wife. You want to talk about revenge? I could have done the same to you, but I didn't. Yes, I signed the loan thing without your consent, but my plan all along was for it to be seamless. The convention would pay for itself, and there would be no harm to you at all. Was it a risk? Yes. But it was also my only way of surviving this life together."

"Like I said, flirting. No more. A drink and conversation," Ned says quietly.

"It's your intent that makes me sick. Why didn't you just ask me for a divorce? Why did you have to see her before ending it with me?" I ask.

"You're right. My intent is what is the worst. The idea of revenge in general is what makes it so bad. But I'm changing, and I'm going to change even more. In that conversation with Cam, I felt something. He asked to pray with me, and in that prayer, I saw it all finally for what it was, and I saw myself for who I have been. I asked God for forgiveness, and I'm asking you for forgiveness too. I see now what Cam and Piper have. It's not some fairy tale true love thing. It's their relationship with Jesus, God, and the Holy Spirit. That's why life works for them. That's why they can be human, have problems, and not turn to their human nature to act the way I did. That's what I've been missing, and I finally see it. And Nancy, it's what *we've* been missing."

"Yeah, well *forgive me* if I don't see this at all the way you do," I say.

"I get it. It may take you more time. But the question is, are you willing to go forward as a couple in complete honesty and give us another try?"

A knock on the door makes me jump.

"Sorry, guys, but it is wrap up time for the convention, and we can't do it without you!" Piper says.

"*I'm* sorry, Piper. I didn't mean to abandon you. I'll be right there," I say.

Watching Piper leave, I know I better get my act together to leave the convention goers on a happy note, not the pathetic truth that just landed on me.

"Nancy ..." Ned says.

"Not now, Ned. I have a convention to complete. I couldn't give you an answer right now anyway. This is all too fresh and raw."

"The last time I spoke with Katherine, I made it clear I wasn't going to continue a friendship with her," Ned says.

Well, gold star for you. Husband of the year. How did I end up with Phillip and now Ned? Really, God?

CHAPTER TWENTY-NINE

"he conclusion? The first Nancy Drew convention at the Grand Hotel on Mackinac Island was a tremendous success! The accolades in the newspaper, the attendees' glowing comments and follow-up survey comments, the Grand itself, and we, your committee, all agree—you thought up and pulled off an amazing feat!' Brenda says.

"Thank you, all. Those are such kind words to begin the final meeting of this committee. None of it would have been possible without all of you and your love for Nancy Drew. We had our moments of excitement, for sure … an understatement. Right?" I ask.

"I'm still reeling from everything that happened. I'm so happy Maxwell has fully recovered. When I think of what that poor man went through …" Maxine says. "Thankfully those bumbling scammers put such a tiny amount of rat poison in his tea, it only made him sick. They are all going to jail for different amounts of time because they all knew about it. It was Perry who did the actual poisoning, at least that's what everyone said who turned on him, even Dolly! Perry must have snuck in and poisoned the tea. I think the three stooges were sent into the room to make sure Maxwell drank the tea. Turns out there was a little too much chlorine in that gene pool where those people came from!"

That got a good laugh from everyone.

"If only I hadn't encouraged him to take a big drink of that tea!" I say.

"There's no way you could have known. Your ex, Phillip, is getting justice too. The signature of Carolyn Keene in the book *did* match his. He wasn't savvy enough to have someone else sign it! He's being charged with accessory to a crime. The law says that the accessory can be charged even if they didn't directly participate in the crime. You won't be dealing with his shenanigans anymore, Nancy, because he will be in jail for a while. Even when he gets out, he should be too afraid to pull any more stunts. That's what I've come to understand, anyway."

"You had to become quite knowledgeable in the law quickly, didn't you Maxine?" Gail asks.

"Yeah, I did. I don't fully understand it all, and I'm not sure I explained it correctly, but that's the gist of it. Clear as mud, ladies?" Maxine asks.

"You did great Maxine," Marlene says. "I'm happy you won't be dealing with Phillip anymore, Nancy. That should be a relief. It sounds like he was going to continue to try to disrupt your life, so good riddance."

"I, for one, will not forget Katherine's awkward attempt to be a part of the closing ceremony, and Nancy's insistence that she leave the convention!" Brenda says with a laugh.

"I agree, that brought a smile to everyone's face," Gail says. "The opening remarks, well, okay. But there was no reason for her to push her way into the closing. She wasn't asked and she had no reason to be there."

"She got to have her moment in the spotlight by creating a little scene, but at least she did leave. I think all the Nancy Drew fans are true sleuths who could see through her bravado. She can't complain. She got to swish around with her skirt featuring the magnifying glass and the candles on her shoes! That's probably why she showed up and wanted to make a speech anyway. I used to be able to tolerate her, but lately, she gets on my last nerve," I say. "On a better note, financially, everything has worked out thanks to the higher than anticipated merchandise sales. I had no idea we could make that much by selling it all. We basically broke even, which means I don't foresee making this an annual event," I say.

Yes, the gals groan a bit, but I think I see a glint of relief, too. It was more work than any of us could have imagined.

"Hopefully, someone else will take up the mantle and there will be many Nancy Drew conventions around the country. I'm happy to lend advice in any way I can, and if there's one I can attend, I'd love to," I say.

"Me too. Maybe we will find one somewhere interesting, and we can all go together!" Brenda says.

"That would be really fun. We could just enjoy it and let someone else experience all the behind-the-scenes trauma. On the other hand, I would do it all over again, even with the problems, just to work with all you wonderful ladies. And thank you to Piper for letting us meet here. Thank you, Sister Mary Margaret, for taking your time off to work with us. You're as wonderful as Piper said you would be, and it's been my pleasure to get to know you," I say.

"Thank you, Nancy, and all you ladies. It's a furlough I won't forget! And yes, Piper is gifted in the art of hospitality. Thank you for including me in this wonderful adventure," Sister says.

"Remember, ladies, we still have our art classes, and Bible studies ... we will stay close for sure. And Sister is so good about keeping those letters coming," Piper says.

"With all those lovely thoughts, that concludes our convention committee meetings," I say, handing out an envelope to each lady. "This is a small token of my appreciation for you to enjoy in a way that makes you happy."

The least I could do was to give each lady a $50 stipend for a little treat. After the usual chatter and sentiments, it's hard to see the ladies leave. Turning to Piper and Sister Mary Margaret, I feel the weight of this ending as it relates to my next steps. For the past two weeks since the convention was over, Ned and I have spoken only when necessary, each of us afraid to start the next conversation. He's been kinder than usual, but quiet. Maybe we know our next real talk could be the one that ends our relationship.

"Nancy, I'm sad to say Sister Mary Margaret is leaving in two days," Piper says, putting her arm around Sister.

"No! I thought we had more time to hang out! I've spent so much time inundating you with everything Nancy Drew, I didn't get to learn more about you," I say.

"It's been my pleasure, and you will be in my prayers in all your future endeavors. Don't say 'never' to another convention. Probably not next year, but in the years to come, who knows?" Sister says with the giggle that lights up the room.

"And, because Sister Mary Margaret has to head out a few days sooner than we thought, we are having a little going away dinner tonight and we'd love it if you would come," Piper says.

"Oh, yes. Please do!" Sister says.

"That actually sounds very nice, I'd love to," I say.

"It will be just us, Freddy—and I promise we'll limit his puns —and you and Ned," Piper says.

"Oh, Ned's invited? Um ..." I say, now sorry I said yes so fast.

"Cam invited him. They've become really close, just as we feel close to you," Piper says.

"Piper, and I guess you might as well know, Sister, Ned and I aren't getting along very well, and basically avoiding one another. So, maybe a dinner party isn't a good idea," I say.

"The focus will be on Sister, really, and Cam will mostly likely monopolize Ned ... we won't let it get uncomfortable, I promise," Piper says. "Is he still mad about the convention? It all worked out and he didn't have to take a financial hit, so surely, he can let that go."

"Confidentially, there's more. That's still a sticking point, but he confessed to me he had a little 'thing,' I guess you would call it with the last person in the world I would want him too ..." I say.

"Oh, Nancy. Not ..." Piper says.

"Yes. Her. Everyone's favorite ... the one who considers herself the queen of the island ..." I say.

"Katherine Sims-Dubois!" Piper and Sister say in unison.

"Nancy, how horrible. Is it in the past?" Sister asks.

"Yes, at least he says so. According to him it was nothing more than flirting, but the very idea that he would do such a thing, especially with her," I say, feeling the pain in my heart all over again. "Actually, if the whole fiasco hadn't happened at the convention, he might have pursued it further. He says he's sorry, and he did it to get revenge on me. How can I forgive that?"

"Forgiveness is hard, isn't it? He had to forgive you; you have to forgive him ..." Sister says.

"No, I don't. I *don't* have to forgive him. I haven't decided yet if I'm going to," I say.

"You're right. It's a tough one, and much more intimate than forgiving something to do with money. It's a matter of the heart. It's all a mess, right?" Sister asks.

"You can say that again," I say.

"Well, Jesus is the only one who can handle messes, whether we cause them or we are at the other end of the stick. You might think, what do I know about being married ... but the issue isn't the marriage. The issue is forgiveness. Whether you and Ned stay together, you're still going to want to forgive him. It's not what it will do to him, but what it will do to you to hold onto all that icky stuff in your heart," Sister says.

It's a preachy girl sermon!

"God knows how we are wired, and He tells us to get rid of anger. He promises a better way of life. Do you really see a future in the path you are going? Do you see peace?" Piper asks. "Of course, you want boundaries of right and wrong in your relationship, but didn't Ned apologize? Didn't he do the right thing after making such poor choices?"

I hate it when she's right.

"Yes, he did. Can we lay all our cards on the table? I was almost happy in a weird, strange way that he did something so horrible I could feel justified in hating him. I've been so mad at him for not being the husband I thought I was getting. I went from one unhappy marriage into something I thought would be good. A super disappointment. Ned is no con man like Phillip, but I still feel abandoned, alone, and duped by not getting what I thought I was getting."

"It's good to express how you feel. God wants your honesty. What if you trusted God's desire for you to trade your anger for forgiveness and, in exchange, you leave justice and mercy up to Him? You could experience peace and freedom, knowing the absolute best outcome for you is ahead, ultimately, because you walk in His ways. Every situation has a choice. We can give our hearts to God, the Creator of the Universe who knows everything all the time about everything. Or we can keep on with the idea that we know how life is supposed to go, and God simply isn't getting it right. That's pretty much the choice we all end up in, and only one leads to peace," Sister says.

Drat! I hate how much they both make sense.

"Here's the truth. God is good and He will ultimately set things right. Where do you want to be in that story?" Piper asks.

As the tears stream down my face, I don't know what I think. This going it alone my whole life hasn't worked.

"That verse in John, Chapter Three, Verse Sixteen ... with a little paraphrasing on my part ... God so loved Nancy, Mary Margaret, and Piper that He sent Jesus, and if they would believe in Him, they would not perish, but would have everlasting life. And the next verse goes on to say that God didn't send His son into the world to condemn it, but to save the world through Jesus. You have been trying to live your life without taking that truth into your heart—giving your life to the One who truly loves you more than any husband or any person on Earth ever could. No wonder you are so disappointed!" Sister says.

"Piper, I'll say it again. Cam isn't like Ned. He's there for you ..." I say.

"Nancy, there is no man that will fill the hole in your heart Jesus was meant to fill. No man, no job, no friendship, no hobby ... you get the picture. Nothing will fill what only *He* can. Cam is a very nice person, but as humans, there are no two people who don't have the honeymoon end, the best behavior end, and go back to being humans who can easily hurt one another. I don't find my fulfillment in Cam; I find it in Jesus. Cam is a nice addition, but when I start thinking he can fill the space that Jesus is meant to fill, it all falls apart. Same thing for him if he thinks I can fulfill him as only God, Jesus, and the Holy Spirit can," Piper says.

"I mean, giving yourself to God ... Shouldn't you feel like, I don't know ... super spiritual ... like the hallelujah chorus strikes up and the room glows ... or ... you know what I mean. I'm not trying to be sarcastic," I say.

"Whether or not you feel like God is around doesn't alter the reality that He is. Even if you're not sure He loves you, that He promises grace and mercy for all of us ... that doesn't change anything. It's all true," Piper says.

"You preachy girls! You're getting to me!"

More tears.

"Anything in your spirit is not us convincing you. That's the Holy Spirit doing what only He can do...making truth known to you. And then, that decision of choosing Jesus or not, that's between you and Him. Keep praying, keep reading your Bible, keep asking...it's no coincidence that we've all been brought together for this moment," Sister says.

"There are no coincidences, only God moments if we will see them for what they are," Piper adds.

"What if I do this, and I don't want to go to church?" I ask.

"Church doesn't save your soul. Church is for our encouragement, and friendship, and joy … and learning more about our faith. I wouldn't be surprised if you found a natural desire for church once you choose Jesus. Remember, it's one step at a time. Just ask God about what you should do next, where you should go next. He will answer you," Piper says.

"Listen, I've taken up enough of your day. Thanks again for everything you did for the convention, the dinner invitation, and for allowing me to use up the entire rest of your box of tissues! I think I'm going to go home now, take a hot bath, and take a nap. I will probably see you later, but please don't be offended if I don't come to the party. It's been quite a few days," I say, standing up to leave.

"Just know how much we hope you do," Piper says, giving me a hug.

"I hope this isn't goodbye, Nancy. I'd love to see you tonight," Sister says, also giving me a hug.

Walking home, I don't notice the tourists or the displays in the windows. I keep seeing the sky and the fluffy white clouds. Are you there, God? Did you do all this? Is what they said real?

"People who daydream when they walk can run into poles, you know!"

Oh, no. Once again, I missed the swishing coming my way. Once again, it's her.

CHAPTER THIRTY

"*H*aving a *tête-à-tête* with your gaggle?"
Katherine Sims-Dubois, who always thinks she's the smartest person in the room just used that phrase incorrectly. A *tête-à-tête*, Katherine, is a private conversation with two people ... like the one I don't want to have with you right now.

"Katherine, I really don't have time for you today. I have places to be, and this is not one of them," I say, starting on my way.

"Not so fast, Miss High and Mighty. You think you put a dent in my day when you refused to let me say my closing remarks at the convention? Well, you are wrong. Those people missed out. That is all. You did them a disservice by robbing them of the best speaker they could ever hear. But don't worry. I have my ways of making sure people who cross me get what they have coming to them."

"Oh, just like how you tried to meddle in my marriage?"

"It takes two to tango, and sweet Ned is so good at, shall we say...tangoing!"

"He told me it was simply conversation, some flirting, and a

165

drink. Happens all the time between people, and it doesn't mean what you think it does," I say wishing once again I could slug her. "And he assured me you won't be seeing him again, so that's the end of it. You had *your* little *tête-à-tête* , so stay away from my husband!"

"Ah, neglected Ned. Seems he wouldn't be seeking out other friendships if he had a woman who could keep him from having a wandering eye, but then. I mean. It's you. Poor, plain Nancy. All swept up in her little mystery club instead of paying attention to her husband. What did you expect? When a beautiful woman gives him a little attention, he's right there with a big smile. He's so good looking; what was I to do when he sought me out? A lady only has so much willpower when it comes to those dimples..."

"Shut up, Katherine!"

People are staring and I don't care.

"Did your little friends invite you to church to join their cult? Aren't they just the preachiest bunch of ladies you ever met? Jesus this and Jesus that. The truth is, the Lord helps those who help themselves, and you, poor Nancy, need some real help. Tah. I've got things to do, people to see."

"Stay away from me and my husband. We want nothing to do with you!"

"Funny you should mention that when I just left a coffee date with sweet Ned. Oh, but then, you left him alone again, didn't you? Yes, we just had coffee, and you had no idea. Best you keep busy, dear. Others will attend to darling Ned, with pleasure."

I know my mouth has dropped and people are staring, but I can't utter a word as she swishes away down the street. Turning and heading home, I don't want to look at anyone's face. All I want to do is get my suitcase packed and get off this island!

Fool me once, Ned. Fool me once. What a liar! Telling me he'd never see her again ... and he's out having coffee with her already, when he knew I would be busy with my last committee meeting. See God? See why I can't do this anymore? See? See how the last piece of hope I had has completely disappeared?

CHAPTER THIRTY-ONE

I bet I look like one of those cartoon animals where steam is coming out of their ears. Anger! Piper and Sister Mary Margaret, you want to see some anger? You should see me now and my beet-red face.

Where is that blasted big suitcase? I'll take all the things I can and then I'll arrange to come back when he's not home to get more. I'll ... I'll ... wait. Where am I going to go? Penny's couch! That's where I'll go, to Traverse City. It's the least she can do for me after giving so much information about me to Phillip.

Crummy men. I probably should tell Piper I'm not coming tonight, but she can figure it out. I'll call her in a few days when I get settled. Maybe she and Cam can help me get more of my things to Traverse City.

"Nancy, are you home?"

Oh, great. I thought I could get out before he got back from ... from his tryst. Wait, I hear more than his voice. Oh, no. I can't take seeing someone else right now.

"Um, can't talk right now, in the middle of something. Sorry!" I yell.

"This will just take a minute. I want you to meet someone," Ned yells back.

Should I make another scene for island gossip with whomever he has brought here, or do I just play along, and wait for whomever it is to leave? Can a day have more drama? Heading out toward the kitchen, I see a tall, lanky man with graying temples smiling at me.

"Nancy, this is Pastor Warren. He's the pastor at the church Cam and Piper go to. He wanted to see my workshop, so I invited him over after we had a meeting today," Ned says.

"Nice to meet you, Nancy. I understand you are the master-mind behind that wonderful Nancy Drew convention I heard so much about. The ladies on your committee couldn't stop talking about how great it was, and how happy they were to work with you," he says, putting out his hand.

I give a quick handshake, just wanting the niceties to end and to get back to packing. I can sneak out while they are in the workshop. I'll call for a horse taxi and have them meet me on the way to the ferry.

"Yes, it turned out well. Piper and the gals are a talented group of women. I was fortunate to have them on my commit-tee. Well, sorry to seem in a hurry, but I'm in the middle of something, and I should get back to it. Enjoy the workshop," I say, turning to leave.

"Nancy, Pastor Warren came with me today to meet with Katherine," Ned says abruptly, looking for my response.

"Oh, I know you were with Katherine. She let me know right in the middle of Main Street with lots of people watching that in no uncertain terms you had a wonderful meeting together. I guess I didn't know the church condoned such happenings though. I'm a little surprised about that," I say, glancing at Pastor Warren.

"No, Nancy. You have it all wrong. I asked Pastor Warren to go with me to make it very clear to Katherine that I was ashamed of my intentions, and to apologize for making a mess of what should have been a cordial but fleeting greeting with a fellow townsperson. I've been meeting with Cam and Pastor Warren to fix this big mess I've made in our lives. They've been helping me to see I need God in my life. I was righting a wrong, and then I've been getting counseling on how to right all the wrongs I've committed against you. I want you to know how sorry I am, and I hope you will forgive me," Ned says, touching my arm.

"I should leave you two alone to talk, but Nancy, what Ned says is true. He didn't want anything to look out of place, so he asked me to go along to meet Katherine, and to do it in a place where there were plenty of people," Pastor says.

"Oh, because you don't trust yourself with the allure of her beauty and charm?" I ask, looking at Ned. "Sorry, Pastor, but I'm a little miffed right now."

"Absolutely not. I want to change and do things the right way. I've given my heart to Jesus. I prayed and asked Him to come into my life. For the first time, I'm understanding God loves me and has a plan for my life. I want accountability and guidance on how to do this Christian thing. Cam and I have been having Bible studies in the workshop, not working on wood projects. I asked Cam to come with me to see Katherine, so she knows for sure it was a big mistake, but he said to bring Pastor Warren," Ned says.

"Just wanting to change out of sheer willpower doesn't work, but when you want to change because you have the Holy Spirit to guide you and to live a life where you have a real relationship with Jesus, that's a miracle. I see it all the time for anyone who gives their life to Him," Pastor Warren says. "I believe Ned is authentic in his desire to know and serve God. I hope that helps you know he's telling you the truth. Listen, Ned, I'll see the shop another time. You and your wife need to talk. Please know you are both more than welcome at church, and more than welcome to come and talk with me anytime. None of us are perfect, and we need a community of people supporting us through choppy waters. I know my wife and I have benefited greatly from seeking Godly counsel in our marriage. It's always available to you. Nice to meet you, Nancy, and you'll both be in my prayers."

A pastor and his wife talk to someone else about marriage. As if.

"I'll see you out the door, Pastor," Ned says.

It's just like Katherine to not tell me the whole story of meeting with Ned, but to say just enough to upset me. She's such a weasel! Now, what do I do?

"Honey, what can I do for you?" Ned asks.

"I don't know, Ned. I was packing when you came home. I was leaving you. I still might," I say, looking at the floor.

"I wouldn't blame you. I wouldn't. But would you please stay awhile longer, and see if we can work this out? If we ever come to the point we can't, I'll help you get on your feet, I will. Honestly, I didn't think it was ever possible that someone as set in their ways and miserly as me could ever be loved by God. But now that it's happened, I see the world differently. I'm blown away by what God did for me, when I was just like the people who were mocking Him on the cross. I don't deserve His love, and I don't deserve yours. Imagine if we *could* work this out. Imagine a husband who puts you first, and listens to you, and supports you in ways that are important to you. Isn't it worth waiting to find out?"

"This whole God thing. Piper and Sister Mary Margaret have been saying the same stuff to me. If they weren't the most genuine, loving people, I would think they were all fanatics. But they're real. They say they are this way because of Jesus in their lives. I don't know what to think. I mean, Piper gave me a Bible and is always bugging me to read a chapter called John," I say.

"That's what kind of started it for me. I read the one Cam gave me, really read it. The more I talked with Cam the more I understood we all have a choice to make ... to live for ourselves in our own selfish ways, or to live for God in His ways. I have to admit, my life hasn't been working. I finally see how selfish I can be. I'm ashamed. I see how I've treated you, too. I'm so sorry, Nancy."

"I can't take one more disappointment. Phillip was a disappointment, and frankly, Ned, you have been, too. And I'm the biggest disappointment of all," I say. "Oh man, look at the time. We are supposed to be at Sister Mary Margaret's going away party soon. She has been such a help to me. I'm not in the mood for this, but I feel like I owe this to her and Piper. Can we not talk about this tonight? Can we just go and be polite, give our best wishes, and be done?"

"Yes. We can do that. But, honey, will you keep an open mind about me and God and the whole thing, and not make any hasty decisions? Will you stay for at least awhile and not take off when I'm out of the house?" Ned asks.

Hmmm.

"I have to get changed. You do, too," I say.

"Nancy?"

"We're not talking about this tonight, remember?" I say, turning toward the bathroom to get ready.

"I love you."

"I wonder what they're serving tonight. We don't have anything to bring," I say, moving closer to the bathroom.

"I've got that block of good Wisconsin cheese. We can bring that," he says.

"Yes, that will work," I say, finally making it to the bathroom and shutting the door.

Looking in the mirror I don't know if I recognize the girl looking back. She has become a mystery to me. God, are You who they say You are? Or is this yet one more quirky path to take until the next disaster strikes and people reveal their true selves? I wish I was sure as the others. There's one big difference between us. They all read the book of John, and I haven't. I'm not sure I want to.

CHAPTER THIRTY-TWO

"*T*hat is a big block of cheese!" Cam says. "You have to take some back home with you. We can't let you share all that Wisconsin goodness with us."

I'm hoping Ned stays true to our plan. I don't want to talk about us. This party should be all about Sister Mary Margaret. Settling into Cam and Piper's cozy living room, I realize how much I'm going to miss these people. Piper and Cam, Sister Mary Margaret, and good 'ole Freddy.

"We are happy to share it. I've got a buddy in Wisconsin and every once in a while, he graces me with his latest favorite cheese. In return, he gets some Mackinac Island fudge. It's a nice trade," Ned says.

"You know, I once heard of a knight who would fight using only a block of cheese. The legends say it was extra sharp," Freddy says with his signature chuckle.

"Freddy, remember what we talked about," Piper warns.

"Yes, Pip, I'll behave. I know Sister Mary Margaret is going to want some simple jokes to take back with her to Africa, so this one is short and sweet," Freddy says. "Did you know, it was a terrible summer for Humpty Dumpty? But it's okay, he had a great fall."

Oh, how I love to hear them all laugh and enjoy the moment.

"Freddy, that one is short enough for me to remember. I have a friend, Sister Albertina, who will love that one. I'll make sure she knows it came from you," Sister Mary Margaret says in her usual, gentle voice.

"You know what I always say. A pun is not completely matured until it is full groan," Freddy says with his expectant gaze at each face as his words sink in.

On cue, we do groan.

"Okay, Freddy. Thank you for the entertainment. Now, as your reward, would you say a prayer for our food?" Piper asks.

"You bet, Pip. Dear Jesus, thank you for each precious person gathered here. They bless me immensely and I pray you bless them. Thank you for this food. Please be with Sister Mary Margaret as she shines her light in Africa. Give her a safe journey and send your angels to protect her and keep her until we meet again. In Jesus' name, Amen."

"Thank you, Freddy. Now everyone, see that spread on the coffee table which now includes some sliced Wisconsin cheese? Please take a plate and help yourself. I thought we would keep it casual and easy and eat right here in the living room. Don't be shy, please dig in," Piper says. "Sister, as the guest of honor, you go first. Oh, and for dessert, there's three kinds of fudge. Try them all. There's German chocolate, if you're a fan of coconut, pistachio with white chocolate, and peanut butter fudge. Everyone get a piece of peanut butter before Cam gets near it, right, honey?"

"She knows me. That peanut butter fudge doesn't stand a chance with me in the room, and I know Freddy will be right behind me," Cam says with a pat on Freddy's shoulder.

They seem to dwell in peace, these people. I've heard tidbits of all their stories, and they've all had their share of trials in life. Unlike me and Ned, they don't limp along like wounded animals. I can't deny there is something different.

As we grab plates and dig into the pinwheel finger sandwiches, tuna salad with peas, veggies with what looks like a wonderful cream cheese dip, fresh fruit, and assorted crackers alongside the cheese from Ned's friend—I hope we can eat and quietly excuse ourselves. I feel weak from it all. Maybe I'm hungry. When was the last time I ate?

"Are you going straight back to Africa, Sister Mary Margaret?" Freddy asks.

"Yes, Freddy. It's quite a trip. It's Detroit, then Amsterdam, then Nairobi," Sister says.

"What do you do in Africa?" Ned asks.

I guess I never asked her either.

"I work with my order in the Kibera slum. It has an interesting history. The Kenyan government owns all the land even though it doesn't officially acknowledge the settlement. There are no basic services, schools, clinics, running water or bathrooms provided, so there is no shortage of a need for help. We try to be the hands and feet of Jesus in a place that is often ignored. When we arrive every day, we are swarmed with little children who want hugs, food, and love. I haven't had one day that I didn't fall into bed exhausted, yet still so satisfied that the love of Jesus was given through water, a hug, or some food," Sister says.

Wow. How do your days hold up to that, selfish Nancy?

"That's amazing work you are doing. Makes my day-to-day seem pretty unproductive!" Ned says.

I'm thinking the same thing.

"You know it's funny. I don't tell everyone what I do when I'm on furlough because it sounds so, well, spiritually exciting. It is. It's also not the call God has for everyone. It's what God laid out for me to do, and He lays out something for every single person who loves Him that is the right fit for them. That's how well He knows each of us. So even if all of you left with me for Africa, and God didn't call you to that—it would be a huge mistake! There is no cookie-cutter approach to each of us. He knows the very number of hairs on our head. Ephesians 2:10, verse Ten says that we are God's handiwork, created in Christ Jesus to do good works, which God prepared in advance for us to do. It's that simple. I'm pursuing what He has for me, and all you have to do is what He prepared for you," Sister says.

"And it brings to mind that wonderful verse from Jeremiah —where God tells us that His plans are to prosper us, and not to harm us," Freddy says. "See, I know more than puns!"

That brings a good laugh from the group.

"I love the promise in John that reminds us Jesus is the vine, and we are the branches. If we stay connected to the vine, we will bear fruit, but apart from Him, we can't do anything," Cam says. "That makes it pretty clear. I stay connected to Jesus, and He gets it done. It's nothing I can do."

"Exactly, Cam. No one is effectively working in Africa or shining their light here on Mackinac Island unless they stay connected to the vine. I think of that with every grape I eat," Sister says, popping one into her mouth.

Ned's eyes are shining.

"Nancy, are we getting preachy again?" Piper asks me.

"Honestly, can you stop yourself?" I ask.

Laughter. It's not nervous laughter, but joyful and accepting. We don't think alike, but I like them so much.

"I've learned a lot from you preachy girls in the last few months. And Sister Mary Margaret, it's been such a wonderful thing to meet you, and learn more about what you do. I hope we can stay in touch," I say.

"We absolutely can. Piper can give you my address. It takes some extra stamps, and it takes a while to get to me and me to write back, but I will always answer. Thank you for including me in the convention. It was so much fun, and being a Nancy Drew fan from way back, I learned tons," Sister says with a wink.

"Preachy girls! Ha! I think I have a new nickname for Piper ... preachy girl," Cam says.

"Yeah, I think a lot of people probably think that, but

haven't said it out loud. I hope to be a preachy girl, but always with love," Piper says with a giggle. "When I think of the wonderful people I've met being that preachy girl ... what adventures!"

"I'm pretty crazy about you, preachy girl," Cam says, kissing her cheek.

"I'm pretty crazy about your tuna salad," Freddy says, scooping up another helping.

"I'm pretty crazy about this Nancy Drew loving gals of mine too," Ned says taking my hand.

I hope they don't see me pull my hand away.

"Hey, it's time to try that fudge ... what were those flavors again?" I ask, turning to Piper.

"That reminds me, what did the hot fudge say to the ice cream? See you next sundae!" Freddy says.

"Freddy!" Cam and Piper say, both rolling their eyes. I'm glad. Freddy did see, and he saved me from an awkward moment once again.

Here's a thought. Maybe I'll be a stowaway in Sister's luggage. Going to Africa sounds better than going home to Ned.

CHAPTER THIRTY-THREE

*J*t was an ugly scene. At least I held it together until we got home. I wanted to let him have it at the party. He's lucky I waited.

How dare he take my hand after what he did. His gesture made it easier to make the call to Penny in Traverse City when he went to his workshop. When he saw I was leaving, he asked me not to go. He asked where I intended to go, but I didn't answer him. Forget it. That's my business.

I'm a little disappointed after talking to Penny to find out she'll be gone to a convention by the time I get there but relieved she's having the super let me in and give me a key. It's a place to start and a way to get away from here.

Catching the Greyhound in Mackinac City, my head hurts from so much to consider. Now that it seems more real, I hope I'm doing the right thing. At least I'll have time to myself on this ride. Greyhounds are good for that. This old bus also makes me think of the "America" song by Simon and Garfunkel ... love that song and their *Bookends* album. Ned and I listened to it all the time when we were dating—back when we were happy.

Ned...can I ever trust you again? Man, this bus is getting

crowded. How many people need to get to Traverse City? Please, don't fill up. I don't want to share a seat.

Oh, good. That grizzly looking guy kept going. So did the lady with the baby. That's all I need, a screaming baby when I'm trying to think. Looks like I might make it, only moments until we pull out again.

"Is this seat taken?"

Seriously? A nun! A nun wants to sit with me? What did I do to meet so many nuns in such a short time?

"Uh ..." I say, hoping she picks up on the drift that I wish she wouldn't.

Why is she wearing a habit? I thought they didn't have to do that anymore.

"I'm sorry, but the bus does seem very full. There must have been a convention or something. I'd prefer to sit with a lady if I could," she says, looking at the few empty seats left including the one next to the man in front of us.

That guy looks more like he should be riding the rails instead of a Greyhound. He smells like it, too.

"Yes, sit down. No problem," I say, moving over to make sure I'm not on her seat.

Finally, we're leaving. This *is* a squeaky old bus. I'll close my eyes. That should be a strong hint I don't want to talk.

"Hey! That's my favorite book, too," she says as I reluctantly reopen my eyes in time to see her wink. "I'm sorry, I didn't introduce myself. I'm Mary Clare."

"I'm Nancy. You're *Sister* Mary Clare, I presume."

"Yes, but I don't insist on it. It kind of weirds some people out," she says quietly so only I can hear.

"More than wearing a habit when I thought you don't have to anymore?" I say.

I probably offended her with that "anymore" part.

"I tend to wear it more when I travel. It might be silly, but it helps me feel safer."

She's younger than me, more Piper's age.

"You like my book? What book?" I ask.

"That Bible I see peeking out of your duffle bag there. It looks like the New Testament I have. I've been spending my time in the book of John lately. Aren't you amazed by the people who think they don't want to be Christians, but they never took the time to read the Bible before they decided. So silly. Am I right?" Mary Clare asks.

"Yeah, what a mistake," I say.

She doesn't know me enough to know my fake voice. Wow. All those preachy girls who don't believe in coincidences would love this.

"To tell you the truth, I've barely begun to read it myself. I was given it by a friend, and I didn't even know it was in my bag," I say.

Ned! Ned must have put it there! He must have seen it on my nightstand and stuck it in my duffle bag. I left so fast I didn't even notice it.

"What I love about it is how John's words show anyone who doesn't believe in Jesus why they should consider Him. John tells about His life, death, and resurrection. It's also for those who may have believed but are struggling with their faith. John hits everyone. Am I right? And there is this amazing, absolutely ah-mazing verse that should blow everyone away! Here, grab your Bible and let me show you ..." Sister Mary Clare says.

I don't think I have much of a choice here.

"Here you go," I say.

"Okay, let's see ... here is Matthew, Mark, Luke ... and yes, John. Now ... let's skip to the very last verse. Are you ready for this?" she asks.

She gets even more excited about the Bible than Piper if that's possible!

"Here it is. It says: 'Jesus did many other things as well. If every one of them were written down, I suppose that even the whole world would not have room for the books that would be written.' Isn't that wild? Picture it! He did so many things that they wouldn't fit in all the books in all the world! That's our Lord! That's who we love and serve. Wow!" Sister Mary Clare says with an exhilarated sigh.

"Yes, that is quite a thing. Uh, back to you being a nun. I can't get over the fact I left a going away party with another nun mere hours ago. I've never had a conversation with a nun in my life before I met her and here you are, nun number two in as many days. Maybe your paths have crossed. Her name is Sister Mary Margaret. She used to be at St. Anne's on Mackinac Island a few years ago before she took her next assignment in Africa," I say.

"Mackinac Island? Believe it or not, I went once as a kid and haven't been back even though it's so close. My order is in California. I was visiting friends in Petosky, popped over here for a day to visit another friend, and now I'm on my way back to Detroit to catch my flight home. I was supposed to have a ride from here, but it fell through. Some people. Am I right? I guess you and I had a divine appointment," she says, nudging me with her elbow.

"The preachy girls, that's what I call my friend who gave me the Bible and her friend, Sister Mary Margaret—anyway—the preachy girls say there are no coincidences in life. Only God moments that we need to pay attention to," I say.

"Yeah, that sounds spot on."

"They just helped me put on a huge Nancy Drew convention at the Grand Hotel."

Why am I all of a sudden telling this nun my life story?

"Nancy Drew? Are you kidding me? I love Nancy Drew! I grew up reading those books. The preachy girls you called them. Ha! I love that. I would like to join that club. I'm a preachy girl myself. Especially when the Holy Spirit is making it very clear about things. So, what's holding you back, Nancy who loves Nancy Drew? You don't want to be a preachy girl?" Sister Mary Clare asks.

"I'm all kinds of confused. I've never given much thought to religion before I met those girls," I say. "Their faith seems to be the most important thing to them, and I don't feel the same way."

"Well, of course you don't. It sounds like you didn't have your own personal meeting yet with Jesus. Am I right? Why would you be excited about Him if you don't know Him?" she asks. "You must be pretty excited about Nancy Drew to go to all the work of having a convention."

"It really was something. All those Nancy Drew lovers together and exploring more about her books and how they came to be. It was great."

"Did you realize your eyes light up when you talk about Nancy Drew? I can see your passion. Now we both know Nancy is a fictional character, yet we can get pretty smiley about those books. Why is it odd when someone gets excited about Jesus? He's real. And when you do get to know Him, He's beyond exciting," she says.

"I guess I never thought about it that way. Until I met those ladies, religion wasn't interesting to me," I say.

"Ever hear the story in the Bible about the lost sheep?"

"No, I don't think so."

"It's a parable Jesus told in the book of Matthew. He's talking about a shepherd, but He's really talking about God. He has one hundred sheep, and one goes missing. He leaves the ninety-nine and searches everywhere for that one lost sheep. When He finally finds it, he's so happy ... even happier about that one sheep than the ninety-nine who never strayed. What I get out of that story is the truth that each person is precious to God. He's always seeking those who don't know Him yet and is full of joy when they are found. He doesn't want anyone to be lost, and that includes you, Nancy. That's why you keep running into all these preachy girls! Could it be that you are the lost sheep?"

"I am lost, I'll give you that. And baaaaaaa. You nailed it. I'm actually on the run from my husband—on my way to bunk with a friend in Traverse City. He did something that hurt me greatly, and I haven't been able to forgive him. He has apologized but every time I think about it, I get so mad, I want to punch him! He flirted with a horrible woman, and she threw it in my face. For the life of me, I don't know why I'm telling you such personal things!" I say.

"Like you're running from an abusive situation?"

"No, nothing like that. He's basically a good guy. I've felt neglected and not seen for the past two years of our marriage—second marriages for both of us. I've been thinking about leaving him, getting divorced, and moving on," I say.

"That is a big decision."

"And get this, as a Nancy Drew lover, you'll appreciate that his name is Ned."

Sister Mary Clare lets out a big laugh.

"Now, that is awesome! Ned and Nancy. He sounds kind of perfect for you. I heard once, and I don't know who said it... probably multiple people in multiple ways ... but I never forgot the meaning; if you focus on the hurt, you will continue to suffer. If you focus on the lesson, you will continue to grow. The bottom line is: we've been forgiven when we didn't deserve it. That's the basis of why we must forgive. Am I right?"

"Yes, the preachy girls made that clear."

"Seems you are in the middle of your own mystery about your life. But Nancy, with all your experience, I also bet you are a master sleuth like our favorite heroine. When you look at the facts, and you look at your heart, you'll get a good answer. I know it. And, on top of that, I'll be praying for you. The Shepherd isn't going to stop looking for you. I guess it's time to decide if you want to be found," Sister Mary Clare says.

Miles are rolling by, and she tells me more Bible stories that have touched her life. She talks about how God exceeds what people thought was possible when they met Him. She would have fit in so well with our team.

"I wish we could keep talking, but I think we are about to

stop in Traverse City. Here's my card with my number and address in California," she says, reaching into her pocket and handing me a business size card. "I had these made so I can keep in touch with the amazing people I meet. If you want to keep in touch, I'd love to hear how *this* Nancy story evolves."

"Good thing you are paying attention. I would probably stay on the bus until they kicked me off. It has been a pleasure talking to you," I say. "I never asked, what do you do in California?"

"I help feed the poor in Los Angeles. We set up lunch every day, mostly donated food, but people are so thankful. There are so many people who need help. Am I right? If you want to be truly grateful for the life you have, I highly recommend helping those who don't have much. It will give you a new perspective on life," she says with a gentle smile. "Well, those screechy brakes mean it's your stop. God be with you, Nancy. I will be praying for you and Ned. It wasn't a coincidence we met. And, hey, I'm joining the ranks of the preachy girls. Let the others know!"

As the bus pulls away, I'm hit with diesel fumes and a wave from someone who has touched my heart immensely. Okay, God. I know I'm dense, but even I am beginning to understand.

CHAPTER THIRTY-FOUR

*F*inding the pay phone in the tiny terminal, I'm hoping it's not too hard to call a taxi in Traverse City to get a ride to Penny's apartment. I must have some change in this duffle pocket.

"Need a ride?"

Turning to that familiar, deep voice, I can't believe my eyes.

"Ned! What ... how... how did you find me and get here so fast?"

"When you left, I thought of Penny and found her number in your address book. I took a chance you took the bus, knowing you're not much for driving. I caught the ferry and borrowed a car from my buddy in Mackinaw City. It's not hard to drive faster than a Greyhound if you speed a little bit. I just made it here a few minutes before you," he says.

"Why did you come? I don't know ..."

"Nancy, being apart is not the answer. I will take this as slowly as you want. We have a home. I love you. I am going to counseling with Pastor Warren to fix the mistakes I've made, and I'm reading my Bible and praying. I'm not perfect, but I'm not the old Ned anymore. I'm committed to this new life, and I'm committed to you. Won't you give us another chance? Even if you want a break, to stay here and have some time to yourself, I want to know you aren't giving up on us!"

He came all this way to find me. Like he was looking for a lost sheep.

"I'm sorry I'm putting you through all this Ned. I believe you are sorry for what happened. I just had a very moving conversation with, can you believe it, another nun! She sat next to me on the bus, and we talked nonstop until I got off here," I say.

"Another nun? That's quite a coincidence. Oops, I recently stopped believing in those," Ned says.

"Me too. There are no coincidences. I finally get it. I'm finally getting so much. I'm ready to go home. We need a real conversation on the drive. Are you okay with that?"

"More than okay. Here, let me get your bag. The car is right outside."

I guess Nancy was right in *The Clue of the Velvet Mask*. When a guy is ready to take a risk for you, he's probably the guy *for* you.

"Funny thing. The Bible Piper gave me ended up in my duffle bag, and I don't think I put it there. Any idea how it got there?"

"I might," he says with a smirk and a touch on the small of my back.

For the first time since the whole Katherine debacle started, his touch feels nice. Going home to our island sounds good. Hanging out with preachy girls sounds comforting. Being who I am called to be, to really be, sounds like the best decision I could ever make.

"It's time to talk, Ned, really talk. It's time to pray."

CHAPTER THIRTY-FIVE

"*T*hen what happened?" Piper asked.

"Ned went back to the gift shop and bought me that cheesy scarf with a picture of the falls. I don't know what I'll do with it, but I couldn't stop talking about it. It was so sweet of him to make sure I had it for a souvenir to bring home," I say.

"It's so wonderful that you guys took a second honeymoon trip to Niagara Falls. So romantic!" Piper says. "Hint, hint, Mr. Cam."

"Hey, Freddy, do you feel like a trip to Niagara Falls? We could go over in a barrel!" Cam says winking at Piper.

"Don't get me in trouble, Mr. Cam," Freddy says.

More laughter at this little get-together at Piper and Cam's house. I've come to love their little bungalow so much and I treasure their friendship.

"Life has changed since I asked Jesus to take over the mess I'd made of my life. On the way home from Traverse City Ned and I prayed together. That chance meeting with Sister Mary Clare on the Greyhound I told you about, and all those conversations with the preachy girls—this lost sheep finally was ready to be found. It's made all the difference in our relationship.

When Ned said he wanted a second honeymoon, I wasn't going to say no," I say.

"We still have our moments, but with our new faith, and the excellent counseling we've been getting with Pastor Warren, we are much better at working through things. We can't thank you enough for speaking up and telling us about your faith. And thanks for hanging in there for all the times we pushed you away. You're faithful friends," Ned says.

"I couldn't have said it better. I'll always love every Nancy Drew story and continue to enjoy the history and part she played in my life, but the real mystery to me is why we are so loved by the God of the universe. He didn't have to do all He did. But He did, sending His Son. Such great love will always be the biggest mystery and I'll never solve it," I say. "I'm so happy to be a part of His story."

"We are all so blessed, so blessed," Piper says softly.

"So blessed to have each other, to be God's children, and to cry, and laugh together," Cam says.

"I'm so glad you brought up the laughter part, Mr. Cam. Because it's been all I could do to hold back some real doozies!" Freddy says.

"Freddy … what did I tell you …" Piper says.

"Freddy …" Cam says.

"Let's hear them, Fred-ster! I love to laugh!" I say.

And for the first time in years, I know the laughter and love are here to stay.

"Okay! So! What do you call Batman after he gets beaten up? Bruised Wayne!" Freddy says with great fanfare.

There are happy groans all around.

"I've got an even better one … did you know, I became hooked on auctions after going once … going twice …"

The End

Here are the titles of the first 50 Nancy Drew novels.
How many Nancy Drew mysteries have you read?

The Nancy Drew Mysteries Series Volumes 1-50

1 *The Secret of the Old Clock*
2 *The Hidden Staircase*
3 *The Bungalow Mystery*
4 *The Mystery at Lilac Inn*
5 *The Secret Of Shadow Ranch*
6 *The Secret of Red Gate Farm*
7 *The Clue in the Diary*
8 *Nancy's Mysterious Letter*
9 *The Sign of the Twisted Candles*
10 *The Password to Larkspur Lane*
11 *The Clue of the Broken Locket*
12 *The Message in the Hollow Oak*
13 *The Mystery of the Ivory Charm*
14 *The Whispering Statue*
15 *The Haunted Bridge*
16 *The Clue of the Tapping Heels*
17 *The Mystery of the Brass-Bound Trunk*
18 *The Mystery at the Moss-Covered Mansion*
19 *The Quest of the Missing Map*
20 *The Clue in the Jewel Box*
21 *The Secret in the Old Attic*
22 *The Clue in the Crumbling Wall*
23 *The Mystery of the Tolling Bell*
24 *The Clue in the Old Album*
25 *The Ghost of Blackwood Hall*
26 *The Clue of the Leaning Chimney*
27 *The Secret of the Wooden Lady*
28 *The Clue of the Black Keys*
29 *The Mystery at the Ski Jump*
30 *The Clue of the Velvet Mask*

31 The Ringmaster's Secret
32 The Scarlet Slipper Mystery
33 The Witch Tree Symbol
34 The Hidden Window Mystery
35 The Haunted Showboat
36 The Secret of the Golden Pavilion
37 The Clue in the Old Stagecoach
38 The Mystery of the Fire Dragon
39 The Clue of the Dancing Puppet
40 The Moonstone Castle Mystery
41 The Clue of the Whistling Bagpipes
42 The Phantom of Pine Hill
43 The Mystery of the 99 Steps
44 The Clue in the Crossword Cipher
45 The Spider Sapphire Mystery
46 The Invisible Intruder
47 The Mysterious Mannequin
48 The Crooked Banister
49 The Secret of Mirror Bay
50 The Double Jinx Mystery

Here are the 17 titles mentioned in this book! How many have you read?

Password to Larkspur Lane
    The Secret of the Old Clock
    The Hidden Staircase
    Nancy's Mysterious Letter
    The Sign of the Twisted Candles
    The Spider Sapphire Mystery
    The Secret of Red Gate Farm
    The Whispering Statue
    The Phantom of Pine Hill
    The Haunted Showboat
    The Mystery of the Moss-Covered Mansion
    The Clue in the Old Stagecoach
    The Secret of the Old Attic
    The Whispering Statue
    The Clue of the Crossword Cipher
    The Clue of the Whistling Bagpipes
    The Clue of the Velvet Mask

Dear Reader,

I hope you enjoyed meeting Nancy Benson and enjoyed all the Nancy Drew trivia throughout the novel along with the beauty of Mackinac Island.

Nancy Benson was very honest with her questions about God and life. These are the types of questions we've all had at some point in our own story. Her questions lead her to the ultimate answer. While Nancy Drew and this story are fiction, there is a forever family that awaits each of us which is very real. That's what life is all about. Do yourself a favor and read the book of John. The book is also about you!

Please stay in touch for the latest news!

Facebook.com/LakeGirlPublishing

My private Facebook team — Piper's Island Peeps:
    Facebook.com/groups/piperpenn

X formerly Twitter @MoDawnWriter

Instagram.com/lakegirlpublishing

Sign up for my newsletter: www.lakegirlpublishing.com/connect
    (I love to hear from readers!)

My email: Info@LakeGirlPublishing

My website: LakeGirlPublishing.com

My heartfelt thanks,

Michèle

Ten Things You Can Do to Keep These Stories Going!

1. **Leave a review**. If you liked the books, leave a kind review. Reviews can be brief, but never give away plot lines or spoilers. Your encouraging words may be the catalyst that introduces someone else to the story — especially important! From Goodreads to all the places books are sold online, your review matters.

2. **Talk about this book on your social media platforms.** Tell your friends that you enjoyed it. Go to other reader Facebook sites like *Avid Readers of Christian Fiction* and sites that love Mackinac Island and recommend my books.

3. **Ask your local library to carry the book(s).** In addition, *Being Ethel (In a world that loves Lucy)* is also available in an audiobook, often popular for library borrowing.

4. **Contact me to speak at your women's group.** Does your women's group need a speaker? I am a speaker for women's and church groups as well as being an author.

5. **Let me know who you are through my website.** Sign up and get my newsletters.

www.LakeGirlPublishing.com/connect

1. **Use these books as gifts!** Email me if you'd like a sticker for the inside of the book, personalized to someone.

2. **Check out my non-fiction book, *5 Easy Steps to a Happy Birthday!*** No adult should ever have a ho-hum birthday ever again.

3. **Pray for me!** I appreciate your prayers! My books have a message of hope and faith, and my desire is to get them to as many people as possible.

4. **Interact with me on social media.** Follow my Facebook.com/LakeGirlPublishing page and my private team's Facebook page, Piper's Island Peeps, for those who are very enthusiastic about my books.
5. **Leave a review!** (No, that's not a typo, it's so important it gets to be on here twice!)

Want a list of questions for your book club to read one (or all) of my books? Send me an email. I'm happy to provide book club questions.

My website: LakeGirlPublishing.com

Thank you for being a part of my team:
Piper Penn's Island Peeps!

Meet Michèle Olson

Michèle Olson has an over forty-five-year career in advertising and marketing as a writer in all mediums, with an emphasis on health writing. She has also enjoyed a professional voice career including time as a DJ (yes, even when they still played records!) and continues to voice local to national commercials and voice projects.

It has always been her dream to segue into fiction and *Being Ethel (In a world that loves Lucy)* was her first in a series based on Mackinac Island — a tiny island in the Straits of Mackinac that connects the Upper and Lower Peninsula of Michigan. A visitor there, along with her husband, for over thirty years, loves to tell people about this unique place with no cars and plenty of fudge!

She is thrilled to share *Being Ethel (In a world that loves Lucy)*, *Being Dorothy (In a world longing for home)*, *Being Alice (In a world lost in the looking glass)*, *Being Wendy (In a world afraid to grow up)*, and this new offering *Being Nancy (In a world lost in mystery)*.

A mom, a mother-in-love, and a "Gee Gee" (G as in good), Michèle resides with her husband in the shadow of Lambeau Field, where life around football abounds. She cherishes her faith and family above all and is delighted to take you on another trip to Mackinac Island, a place that has brought her so much respite and joy.

She loves connecting, so reach back through all the social media links provided.

Stay connected for more stories from Michèle Olson.

www.LakeGirlPublishing.com/connect

**Ten places to explore if you go to Mackinac Island!
(There are many more, too!)**

1. **Arch Rock.** This is a natural rock bridge that sits
   149 feet above the Straits of Mackinac as if it's
   suspended in midair! You can walk there, or you can
   stop as part of a carriage tour. It's fun to see from
   below or up close.
2. **Fort Mackinac.** Known to be the oldest building in
   Michigan, you can see history come alive and
   imagine yourself living in a military outpost. It's the
   fortress on a bluff you see as you come into the
   harbor. Listen at certain times of the day — the
   cannon does work!
3. **St. Anne's Catholic Church.** This beautiful
   church is worth seeing, including the stained glass
   windows. Of course, if you're like me, you imagine
   Sister Mary Margaret sitting in a pew just waiting to
   have a conversation with you.
4. *Somewhere in Time,* the wonderful movie filmed
   on the island in 1979 and part of *Being Ethel (In a
   world that loves Lucy),* my first novel in this series,
   boasts multiple island treasure stops. Seek out the "Is
   it you?" spot with a plaque commemorating the line
   and, of course, the famed gazebo. Relocated from its
   original place in the movie, anyone on the island can
   tell you where to find it!
5. **Fort Holmes**. Do you like to hike? Go to this
   highest point on the island, even higher up than Fort
   Mackinac. Originally named Fort George, it was
   renamed when the Americans returned to the fort in
   1815. In 2015, it was reconstructed for visitors to
   learn more about its amazing history.
6. **Round Island Lighthouse.** You'll pass this
   beautiful lighthouse as you ferry in and away from

the island. Not a spot for visitors, as much as sightseers, you'll find yourself looking for it whenever you are near the shores of the island. It, too, has a pivotal scene in *Somewhere in Time*. Besides, don't you just love lighthouses?

7. **Eagle Point Cave.** Once again, it's for the hiker in you! Located on the north side of the island. When you are there, read about some of the tall tales surrounding this interesting spot.

8. **Sugar Loaf.** It's an adventurous hike or bike ride to make it to this tall geological formation but worth it. How many times have you seen a limestone stack on an island? You see my point!

9. **The Grand Hotel**. Of course! Either go for a stay or pay the minimal fee and walk around for a day. Be sure to sit on that famous porch on a white wicker rocking chair and imagine you are having a conversation with Piper Penn!

10. **The Island Bookstore.** Located inside The Lilac Tree entrance on Main St., this wonderful bookstore has been bringing the best in books to island visitors for decades! You can get a Mackinac Island favorite or browse the wide variety of books available. Stop in and take a picture of my books! **Send me a pic of you there with my book(s), and I'll send you a wonderful treat in the mail!**

Non-fiction by Michèle Olson

5 Easy Steps to a Happy Birthday!
A practical, funny guide to a Happy Birthday every single year!

When was the last time, as an adult, you had a glorious, fun-filled, satisfying, memorable Happy Birthday? If that's not your norm, it's time for a change! Whether circumstances, apathy, or disappointment have pushed you into a world of ho-hum birthdays, this is your chance to recover the bliss of a well-celebrated birthday—on your terms.

Filled with practical suggestions, get ready for an outrageously gratifying, joyous, and "dream come true" birthday—every year. Everyone should have a Happy Birthday, every single year! Get ready to celebrate!

Freebies and More Fun!

Would you like a personalized signed sticker for your book?
 Simply email me. I'll let you know how to get one when you send a Self-Addressed Stamped Envelope. Also, it's a great gift idea!

Are you going to Mackinac Island? Please take some pictures of my book on the island at various places and in The Island Bookstore! Send me some pics of you and fun book pics. I'll send you a special prize!

info@lakegirlpublishing.com

Email me! info@lakegirlpublishing.com
 Check out my art shops: Etsy
 https://www.etsy.com/shop/LakeGirlPublishing

Fine Art America:
 https://www.fineartamerica.con/profiles/2-michele-olson

Need a speaker for your conference? Check out my speaker page at:
 www.LakeGirlPublishing.com/speaker

Keynote and breakout session speaker with Doodling and Sketchnote sessions including teaching others to doodle with joy!

Mackinac Island and the Upper Peninsula of Michigan is a beautiful place to see the dazzling lights that are on the cover postcard and happen as part of the story in *Being Nancy (In a world lost in mystery)!*

The Northern Lights, also known as the Aurora Borealis, happen in regions around the earth's magnetic pole. They appear when electrons from solar flares interact with atoms and molecules in the Earth's atmosphere. That in turn creates lights and multiple colors in the sky.

In the U.P. you are more likely to see the Northern Lights between August and April, with the peak months being April, October, and November. Choose a clear, crisp, chilly night without the threat of lake-effect snow.

Look for my Northern Lights painting on cards and magnets in my Lake Girl Publishing Etsy site. Or email me for info on getting any of my art.

**Looking for some of the Bible verses talked about in
*Being Nancy (In a world lost in mystery)?***

The Message Bible is one of my favorite Bible versions. It was not yet written at the time of this story, but I thought you would enjoy seeing some of the verses in this book as they are expressed in *The Message*. Blessings!

John 3:16-18 *This is how much God loved the world: He gave his Son, his one and only Son. And this is why: so that no one need be destroyed; by believing in him, anyone can have a whole and lasting life. God didn't go to all the trouble of sending his Son merely to point an accusing finger, telling the world how bad it was. He came to help, to put the world right again. Anyone who trusts in him is acquitted; anyone who refuses to trust him has long since been under the death sentence without knowing it. And why? Because of that person's failure to believe in the one-of-a-kind Son of God when introduced to him.*

Matthew 18:21-22 *At that point Peter got up the nerve to ask, "Master, how many times do I forgive a brother or sister who hurts me? Seven?"*
   Jesus replied, "Seven! Hardly. Try seventy times seven."

James 1:5-8 *If you don't know what you're doing, pray to the Father. He loves to help. You'll get his help and won't be condescended to when you ask for it. Ask boldly, believingly, without a second thought. People who "worry their prayers" are like wind-whipped waves. Don't think you're going to get anything from the Master that way, adrift at sea, keeping all your options open.*

Jeremiah 29:11 *I know what I'm doing. I have it all planned out—plans to take care of you, not abandon you, plans to give you the future you hope for.*

Romans 8:26-28 *Meanwhile, the moment we get tired in the waiting, God's Spirit is right alongside helping us along. If we don't know how or what to pray, it doesn't matter. He does our praying in and for us, making prayer out of our wordless sighs, our aching groans. He knows us far better than we know ourselves, knows our pregnant condition, and keeps us present before God. That's why we can be so sure that every detail in our lives of love for God is worked into something good.*

John 14:6 *Jesus said, "I am the Road, also the Truth, also the Life. No one gets to the Father apart from me."*

Ephesians 4:29 *Watch the way you talk. Let nothing foul or dirty come out of your mouth. Say only what helps, each word a gift.*

John 21:25 *There are so many other things Jesus did. If they were all written down, each of them, one by one, I can't imagine a world big enough to hold such a library of books.*

The Parable of the Lost Sheep

Luke 15:1-3 *By this time a lot of men and women of questionable reputation were hanging around Jesus, listening intently. The Pharisees and religion scholars were not pleased, not at all pleased. They growled, "He takes in sinners and eats meals with them, treating them like old friends." Their grumbling triggered this story.*

4-7 *"Suppose one of you had a hundred sheep and lost one. Wouldn't you leave the ninety-nine in the wilderness and go after the lost one until you found it? When found, you can be sure you would put it across your shoulders, rejoicing, and when you got home call in your friends and neighbors, saying, 'Celebrate with me! I've found my lost sheep!' Count on it—there's more joy in heaven over one sinner's rescued life than over ninety-nine good people in no need of rescue."*

Matthew 5:14-16 *"Here's another way to put it: You're here to be light, bringing out the God-colors in the world. God is not a secret to be kept. We're going public with this, as public as a city on a hill. If I make you light-bearers, you don't think I'm going to hide you under a bucket, do you?*

I'm putting you on a light stand. Now that I've put you there on a hilltop, on a light stand—shine! Keep open house; be generous with your lives. By opening up to others, you'll prompt people to open up with God, this generous Father in heaven."

Matthew 11:28-30 *"Are you tired? Worn out? Burned out on religion? Come to me. Get away with me and you'll recover your life. I'll show you how to take a real rest. Walk with me and work with me—watch how I do it. Learn the unforced rhythms of grace. I won't lay anything heavy or ill-fitting on you. Keep company with me and you'll learn to live freely and lightly."*

Revelation 21:27 *Nothing dirty or defiled will get into the City, and no one who defiles or deceives. Only those whose names are written in the Lamb's Book of Life will get in.*

Hey, have you read the Bible for yourself?
The greatest mystery of endless love awaits you!

9 781959 178026